MAD® ABOUT STAR WARS®

WRITTEN BY JONATHAN BRESMAN

DEL REY

Ballantine Books • New York

A Del Rey Trade Paperback Original

Copyright © 2007 by E.C. Publications, Inc.

Published in the United States by Del Rey Books,
an imprint of The Random House Publishing Group,
a division of Random House, Inc., New York.

DEL REY is a registered trademark and the Del Rey
colophon is a trademark of Random House, Inc.

Library of Congress Cataloging-in-Publication Data

Bresman, Jonathan.
Mad about Star wars / Jonathan Bresman.
        p.   cm.
ISBN 978-0-345-50164-6 (pbk.)
1. Star Wars films—Humor.   2. Star Wars films—Comic
books, strips, etc.   I. Mad.   II. Title.
   PN6231.S725B74 2007
   791.43'750207—dc22   2007019853

Printed in China

www.delreybooks.com
www.madmag.com

9 8 7 6 5 4 3

Designed by Ryan Flanders

FOREWORD BY GEORGE LUCAS

I'm a lifelong *MAD* fan.

I remember discovering it as a kid. I grew up in an agricultural town in the 1950s and early 1960s, which was not exactly the place for questioning authority. But then *MAD* Magazine came along. By artfully weaving together intelligent satire and lowbrow laughs, it pulled back the curtain on the adult world. *MAD* took on all the big targets—parents, school, sex, politics, religion, big business, advertising, and popular culture—using humor to show that, more often than not, the emperor, as it were, had no clothes.

This revelation helped me recognize that just because something is presented to you as the "way it is" doesn't mean that that's the way it *really* is. I realized that if I wanted to see a change in the status quo, I couldn't rely on the world to do it for me. The impact this had on my worldview was enormous—an impact that continues to this day. I have spent much of my career telling stories about characters who fight to change the dominant paradigm. I've dedicated decades to changing the way movies are made, and I've established an educational foundation that encourages people to think differently about how to best teach kids. For all that, Alfred E. Neuman bears at least a little of the blame.

Over the years, I have maintained personal contacts with *MAD*. When I had to choose an artist for the *American Graffiti* poster, veteran *MAD* caricaturist Mort Drucker was the first and only person who came to mind. Later, when I saw myself and my work depicted in *MAD*, I wrote to "the Usual Gang of Idiots," letting them know how much of a thrill it was. I even bought the original artwork. (Perhaps most importantly, I have always defended *MAD* from my lawyers.)

If you are an adult reading this book, I hope it brings back fond memories. If you are a kid reading this material for the first time, I hope it makes you laugh as you never have before, and maybe makes you see the world a bit more questioningly. In either case, I hope this book brings you even a fraction of the joy it brought me.

George Lucas
Skywalker Ranch, Marin County, CA
October 2007

CONTENTS

INTRODUCTION BY JONATHAN BRESMAN

In college I had the unusual experience of interning first for *MAD* Magazine and then for Lucasfilm. After college, I went to work at Skywalker Ranch full time. Both places were absolutely insane. At *MAD*, for example, I went through a series of initiation tasks, the most memorable of which was having to glue things to myself until I was too heavy to move. At Lucasfilm I was ordered to run around in a primitive Jar Jar Binks costume while being chased by a pickup truck in order to give George Lucas a "rough idea" of what a scene from *The Phantom Menace* would look like.

I'm not sure which was more humiliating.

These days I'm back at *MAD* Magazine as senior editor, and they don't make me glue things to myself anymore. Instead I get to do dream projects like this one, which gives me the chance to relive a bit of my childhood. Putting together the material for this book led me to reconnect with *MAD* #242, the issue that parodies *Return of the Jedi*. It was the very first *MAD* I ever bought in 1983, when I was nine years old.

Reading it again brought back the exhilaration I felt upon seeing the movie, as well as the rich memory of my first taste of satire. "*MAD* is *so* right!" I remember thinking. "Lucas *was* rehashing the Death Star battle from *Star Wars*!" And of course, I could never forget my first encounter with Don Martin's piercing observation that if the speeder bikes Luke and Leia used could fly, why didn't they just fly above all those trees so they wouldn't have to worry about crashing into them? For a nine-year-old, these were eureka moments.

Beyond mere reminiscing, however, going through thirty years of *MAD*'s *Star Wars* parodies has provided me with a fascinating (and twisted!) look at recent American social, cultural, and political history.

In their 1970s spoofs of *Star Wars*, "the Usual Gang of Idiots" toss off references to Muhammad Ali, *Hollywood Squares,* and *Sesame Street*, an indication of how large each then loomed in the cultural land-scape of the era. Meanwhile, some of the songs parodied in the *MAD* musical "The Force and I," which were still well-known in 1978, are now more obscured with time. (For example, while "By the Time I Get to Phoenix" was a big hit in the late 1960s, it's probably not getting as much airplay today.)

In the 1980s we see gags about Atari, Ronald Reagan's Strategic Defense Initiative (nicknamed "Star Wars"), and, of course, Mr. T. A pretty good summary of that decade—at least by VH1 standards.

In the 1990s, reflecting the tone of the times, *MAD*'s humor coarsens. With the release of the Special Edition of the original *Star Wars* trilogy, *MAD*'s parodies depict Princess Leia performing lap dances, while C-3PO is threatened with the prospect of getting his "nuts" tightened. With society's increased obsession with celebrities, Lucas now transitions from just making cameos in *MAD*'s spoofs and starts to become a central subject of satires himself, a trend that continues in the 2000s. Additionally, with *Star Wars*' renewed status as a cultural touchstone, *MAD* uses it as a vehicle for cultural and political satire, turning out such gems as "*Star Wars* Macarena," and "Starr Wars," a poster mocking Kenneth Starr's investigation of the Monica Lewinsky affair.

In the post-9/11 era, *MAD*'s political satire becomes even sharper. Thus, on the *Star Wars* front, we see "the Usual Gang of Idiots" playfully comparing the title crawl of *Revenge of the Sith* to Bush's State of the Union address. We are also treated to articles like "Startling Similarities between *Star Wars* and the War on Terrorism," and the poster parody "Gulf Wars: Episode II Clone of the Attack" (which made a particularly big splash on the Internet).

Which way the tides of pop culture will carry *MAD* next, though, is anyone's guess. But with George Lucas churning out *Star Wars* TV shows, and the fact that he will probably keep issuing "Special Editions" until the universe dies, *MAD* will likely have Darth Vader and company to keep kicking around for a long, long time.

So whether you're a fan of the Force or the Farce, may they both be with you.

Jonathan Bresman

Jonathan Bresman
MAD World Headquarters, New York, NY
October 2007

DISCLAIMER TO PREEMPT FAN NITPICKING

Both *MAD* and *Star Wars* are blessed with legions of fans who express their love and admiration by obsessively examining every product with an unforgiving eye and then writing rant-filled, accusatory letters whenever they find a "mistake" or "oversight." As a goodwill effort to save these fans the time, we freely admit that this book does not contain *every* last reference *MAD* has ever made to *Star Wars*. For example, we didn't include our *Working Girl* parody, even though we gave Harrison Ford some ribbing by throwing in a minor nod to *Star Wars*. Call us crazy, but we didn't think the fanbase buying this book included many Melanie Griffith groupies.

While we're sure we'll still get complaints about some of the other articles we didn't include, rest assured that this book contains every parody significant enough to be seen. If you still aren't satisfied, then all we can say is that maybe we'll include the stuff we left out in our *next Star Wars* book, thirty years from now. Reserve your copy today!

Thank you.

P.S. Don't even *think* about writing us a letter about how you can't really reserve it today. We know how your little minds work, you nitpicking numskulls!

Illustration by Hermann Mejia.

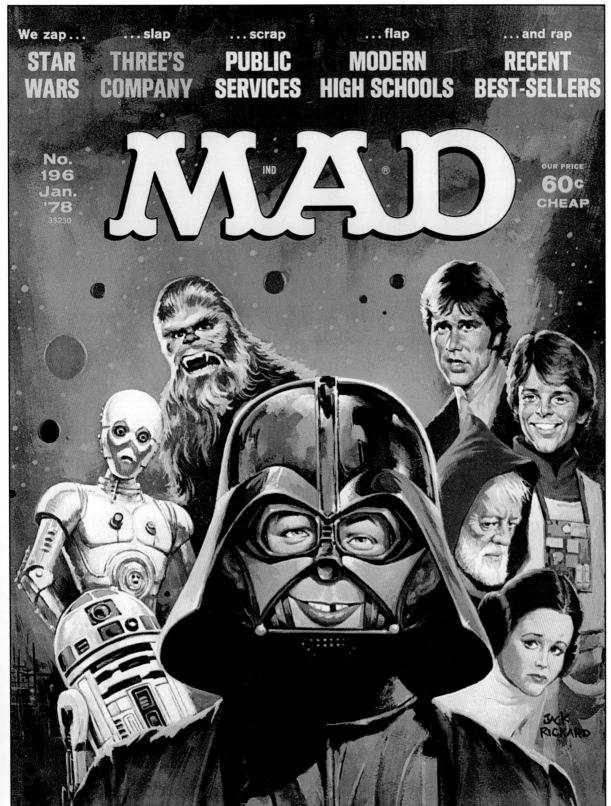

We zap... ...slap ...scrap ...flap ...and rap

STAR WARS   **THREE'S COMPANY**   **PUBLIC SERVICES**   **MODERN HIGH SCHOOLS**   **RECENT BEST-SELLERS**

No. 196 Jan. '78 33230

MAD IND ®

OUR PRICE 60¢ CHEAP

JACK RICKARD

MAD #196, January 1978
Cover, Alfred as Darth Vader
(Artist: Jack Rickard)

LAG TIME
Notice the cover date of January 1978. *Star Wars* came out in May 1977. While it might look like "the Usual Gang of Idiots" works extremely slowly, keep in mind that *MAD* only came out eight times a year in the 1970s. Furthermore, the culture was slower back then, and the way movies were released was much different. *Star Wars* didn't open right away on thousands of screens. In fact, it initially opened in only thirty-two theaters. Also, movies stayed in theaters for much longer. So by 1978 standards, eight months was practically lightspeed.

R2-D2 AS MAILBOX
Note the mail slots on R2-D2 (bottom right). Almost thirty years after *MAD* first thought of it, Lucasfilm and the United States Postal Service finally introduced R2-D2 mailboxes in 2007. We'd say great minds think alike, but neither Alfred E. Neuman nor the postal service has ever been known for mental competence!

An R2-D2-themed mailbox.

MAD #196, January 1978
"Star Roars"

STAR ROARS

ARTIST: HARRY NORTH, ESQ.   WRITER: LARRY SIEGEL WITH DICK DE BARTOLO

Incredible! Our ship goes faster than the speed of light, and our guns fire almost as fast as the speed of light!

Yeah . . . so guess what just happened! We shot ourselves down!!

What?! You mean to tell me that the In-Flight Movie is Bugs Bunny chasing the Roadrunner up a hill?!?

What do you expect on a seven second flight . . . "The Godfather"?

How high up into space would you say this ship goes?

Quiet! I'm about to say a prayer before we go into battle . . .

OUR FATHER WHO ART BELOW US IN HEAVEN—

That high, huh?

Boy, these space ships are noisy!! Maybe that's why they call this movie . . .

We got away, Bar-Stool! So good, so good! The Princess depends on us! Our mission must not fail!

Beedeep! Boop! Tweet!

TRANSLATION: If we're both robots, Cree-Pio, how come we look—and talk—so different?

Because I happen to be a magnificent, articulate golden Adonis, and you're a sawed-off, incoherent, stupid sack of bolts!

Beedeep! Boop!

TRANSLATION: I knew there had to be a scientific reason for it!

Goodness gracious, this planet simply screams for some—Je ne sais quoi—in the way of decor! Still, in some ways, it's a veritable Shangri-La! Take my hand, Bar-Stool . . . I'm a stranger in paradise . . .

Beedeep! Tweet!

TRANSLATION: As if I don't have enough problems, now I'm stuck with a gay robot!

Bar-Stool, we seem to be lost! Oh, dear . . . look what's coming! Fiendish creatures about to tear us limb from limb and commit unspeakable acts of cruelty upon us . . . !

Follow the yellow sand road! Follow the yellow sand road! Follow . . . follow . . . follow . . . Follow the yellow sand road!

Beep! Zit! Gack!

TRANSLATION: And then again . . . there's an outside chance they may be Space Munchkins!

Hi, strangers! I'm Lube Sky-stalker! I'm a senior at Buffooin Tech, where I major in Incredible Space Heroics!

Gracious, there couldn't be any money in THAT field!

You're telling me! That's why I'm minoring in Space Accounting! Hey, anyone ever tell you you look like an "Oscar"?!?

Take a good look! With your performance in this film, it's as close as you'll ever get to an Academy Award!

SHOES IN SPACE
Just as we saw with the R2-D2 mailbox, MAD's parodies have a history of being remarkably prescient of things to come. Notice the shoes floating in space. It took Industrial Light & Magic (ILM) half a decade to catch up with MAD, when the visual effects team slipped a tennis shoe into Return of the Jedi's space battle.

"BOY, THESE SPACE SHIPS ARE NOISY!!"
In an attempt to find the perfect spaceship noise, sound designer Ben Burtt traveled to air bases all over the country, recording the sounds of rockets and missiles. Nothing sounded right. Finally, after a fruitless recording session at White Sands, New Mexico, Burtt returned to his motel room and went to sleep. In the middle of the night he was woken by the sound of the room's broken air conditioner and realized he had found what he was looking for. (As best as we can determine, Lucasfilm never paid a royalty to the air conditioner's manufacturer.)

C-3PO AS "OSCAR"
MAD Magazine wasn't the only one to make the connection between C-3PO and Oscar. In fact, C-3PO made an appearance at the 1978 Academy Awards. Unfortunately for actor Anthony Daniels, once he changed out of the C-3PO outfit and into his tuxedo, security was unable to recognize him in his human identity. They concluded he was a gate crasher and tried to have him arrested.

HOLLYWOOD SQUARES, STAR WARS, AND MAD—LESS THAN SIX DEGREES OF SEPARATION

Bruce Vilanch, a frequent guest on *Hollywood Squares* in the late 1990s and early 2000s, was one of the "writers" responsible for the horrific 1978 "*Star Wars* Holiday Special." This televised abomination was so bad (it starred Bea Arthur and is probably used by the CIA in its secret prisons as a form of torture) that George Lucas once joked that he would destroy every bootleg copy in existence if he could. Unfortunately, there are some things beyond even the power of Lucas, as you can find clips of it pretty easily online. (In the interests of full disclosure, *MAD* must admit that it had Vilanch write the foreword to *MAD About the Oscars*.)

Bea Arthur tending bar as Ackmena in the Mos Eisley cantina.

OSCAR THE GROUCH
Notice the famous Muppet from *Sesame Street* on the immediate left. C-3PO and R2-D2 actually made several appearances on the children's show in 1980. In the course of one episode, R2-D2 falls in love with a fire hydrant. Seriously.

C-3PO and R2-D2 on *Sesame Street*.

"WEIRD THINGS"
George Lucas wrote in his foreword to *The EC Archives: Weird Science Volume 1* that EC Comics, *MAD*'s predecessor publications, had an "indelible impact" on him, and that it's "no coincidence" that, like the *Weird Science* comic, *Star Wars* features monsters, laser beams, robots, and space-ships. Al Feldstein, *MAD*'s editor-in-chief at the time of *Star Wars*' release, was largely responsible for *Weird Science*, and was pleased and honored to learn of its influence on Lucas and the *Star Wars* films.

"EXCUSE ME, BUT I'M FROM THE ELECTRIC COMPANY..."

The man from the electric company in the panel to the right is, of course, George Lucas. He'll turn up a bunch of times before the end of this book. Go figure!

George Lucas in Tunisia, 1976.
© Lucasfilm Ltd. & TM. All rights reserved.

"500 SHARP-SHOOTERS...MISS FROM A DISTANCE OF TEN FEET!"

This comment was truer than *MAD* realized. Sound designer Ben Burtt reports that when he got the initial test animation of the laser bolts from ILM, it was evident right away that the stormtroopers couldn't hit anything—but not for lack of trying. The problem was, the ILM guys put in four times as many laser bolts as there were stormtroopers shooting, and had them going any which way. They also hadn't bothered synching up the lasers with the muzzle flashes of the guns fired on the set, which shot blanks. Even worse, the lasers looked like javelins, and they were moving slowly enough for the intended targets to easily move out of the way. On the other hand, having Luke and Leia shot dead at this point would have made for a much shorter movie.

WHO'S PILOTING THE X-WINGS?

In the Special Edition version of the film, released in 1997, all the computer-generated X-wings were piloted by digital clones of visual effects supervisor John Knoll. (In the panel on the right, however, the X-wings are piloted by Alfred E. Neuman, the Black and White Spies, Roger Kaputnik, William M. Gaines, Richard M. Nixon, Mary Tyler Moore, Charo, Jimmie Walker, Walt Disney's head, and Mahatma Gandhi. Unfortunately, you need exceptionally good vision to see this.) Knoll also got to "fly" a Naboo N-1 starfighter in *The Phantom Menace*. Now, before you whiningly ask what makes *him* so special, you might want to know that he co-invented Photoshop (with his brother, Thomas, no less) and won an Oscar for his visual effects work on *Pirates of the Caribbean: Dead Man's Chest*. What bit of world-changing software have *you* invented lately?!

John Knoll as Naboo N-1 starfighter pilot Rya Kirsch.

MAD MOCKS STAR WARS MERCHANDISE

STAR WARS MOUTHWASH

"I'd Give Up An Empire For It!"

DESTROYS BAD BREATH

R2D2 TRASHCAN

PUSH

HELP KEEP OUR UNIVERSE CLEAN

MARK *Virginia* HAMILL

MAY THE PORK BE WITH YOU!

MORONIC MERCHANDISE

Star Wars became a merchandising monster very early on, and *MAD* delighted in poking fun at the ridiculousness of turning ordinary items into "collectibles." While there is no *Star Wars* Mouthwash nor any Mark Virginia HAMill, Steve Sansweet, Lucasfilm director of content management and fan relations, as well as a prominent *Star Wars* collector, reports that there are indeed high-end R2-D2 trash cans available for purchase in Japan. No word on whether they ever developed a Sarlaac Pit Garbage Disposal.

The items on this page were selected from the following articles: "Merchandising We're Almost Sure to See…and Hate!"—*MAD* #241, September 1983 (*Star Wars* Mouthwash); "*MAD*'s Celebrity Supermarket"—*MAD* #258, October 1985 (Mark Virginia HAMill); and "Merchandising Spin-Offs that Hollywood Missed"—*MAD* #276, January 1988 (R2-D2 trash can).

The R2-D2 trashcan.
Photo by Anne Neumann.

A MAD LOOK AT

SERGIO ARAGONES DEPT.

LIGHTSABER AS FLASHLIGHT

Here Sergio Aragonés makes the connection between light-saber and flashlight, as have countless children around the world. What Aragonés wasn't aware of is that while the original lightsabers were not built from flashlights, they *were* built from another light source: the handle to an old-time flashbulb called a 3-cell Graflex Flashgun—the kind you might see attached to cameras in the 1940s. So, if you want a lightsaber, all you need to do is find a sixty-year-old flashbulb handle—or, you know, go to Toys "R" Us.

MAD #197, March 1978
"A *MAD* Look at 'Star Wars'"

"STAR WARS"

ARTIST & WRITER: SERGIO ARAGONES

CHEWBACCA AND PURINA

Sergio Aragonés didn't know it at the time when he depicted Chewbacca eating Purina dog food, but the Wookiee was actually based on George Lucas's dog, Indiana. The Alaskan malamute used to sit in Lucas's passenger seat, and thus inspired the creation of the canine-like co-pilot. Indiana was also, of course, Indiana Jones's namesake.

A late 1970s photo of sound designer Ben Burtt with George Lucas's dog, Indiana.
Photo by Peg Burtt.

ANOTHER R2-D2/ MAILBOX GAG

MAD apologizes for this pathetic repetition of a gag. Until, of course, they use it again!

LUKE AND THE LAVATORY

This strip, where Luke encounters all sorts of strange urinals, is a fan favorite. In fact, as Lorne Peterson, veteran Industrial Light & Magic model maker, reports, it was even tacked up in the ILM model shop. After all, it answered a basic question that was never addressed in science-fiction films—what kind of bathroom can accommodate so many alien physiologies? To this very day Aragonés *still* gets comments on this classic strip at every comic convention he attends.

HERE WE GO WITH ANOTHER RIDICULOUS
MAD FOLD-IN

Actors come from a variety of places, such as neighborhood theaters, summer stock, local TV, repertory companies, etc. But lately, actors are coming from a really unique place. To find out what that place is, fold in page as shown.

FOLD PAGE OVER LIKE THIS!

"ACTORS ARE COMING FROM A REALLY UNIQUE PLACE."
Here, *MAD* makes a comment on the rise of the visual-effects-generated "actor," not realizing that years later such "actors" would emerge from the digital realm as opposed to the machine shop.

A▶   FOLD THIS SECTION OVER LEFT   ◀B FOLD BACK SO "A" MEETS "B"

ROYAL CROWN THEATER

ARTIST & WRITER: AL JAFFEE

THESPIANS TODAY ARE PLAYING EVERYTHING...FROM MACBETH TO LITTLE ORPHAN ANNIE. WHEN SPOTLIGHTS SHINE SHOW FOLKS WORK TIRELESSLY UNTIL THEY REACH THE TOP

A▶   ◀B

NO NEED TO RUIN YOUR BOOK BY FOLDING THIS PAGE! JUST TURN TO THE NEXT PAGE TO SEE THE ANSWER!

MAD #199, June 1978
Fold-in, "Where Are Some Very Successful Actors Coming from Lately?"

WHERE ARE SOME VERY SUCCESSFUL ACTORS COMING FROM LATELY?

FOLD PAGE OVER LIKE THIS!

A▶◀B FOLD BACK SO "A" MEETS "B"

ARTIST & WRITER: AL JAFFEE

THE MACHINE SHOP

A▶◀B

MAD #199, June 1978
Fold-in FOLDED!

SPECIAL IN THIS ISSUE THE MAD "STAR WARS" MUSICAL

No. 203 Dec. '78

MAD IND

OUR PRICE 60¢ CHEAP

JACK RICKARD

EXCLUSIVE: SCIENTISTS RELEASE FIRST COMPUTER-WRITTEN JOKE

MAD #203, December 1978
Cover, "The MAD 'Star Wars' Musical"
(Artist: Jack Rickard)

TOP HATS

LucasArts producer David Perkinson reports that, in the 2006 video game *LEGO Star Wars II: The Original Trilogy,* there is a hat machine on the Tatooine level. The machine allows you to choose from a variety of hats to put on your character, including top hats and even Princess Leia's famous hairstyle.

Chewbacca doesn't seem too pleased with his top hat. Luke, however, seems to think it's the perfect complement to his stormtrooper disguise.

LUCAS AND DRUCKER

"It has been my pleasure," says Mort Drucker, "to satirize the brilliant *Star Wars* episodes." However, George Lucas and Mort Drucker have an association that actually precedes the *Star Wars* films. Lucas was such a fan of *MAD* and of Drucker's work growing up that he hired Drucker to create the poster for *American Graffiti*. After they were printed, Lucas brought a pile of posters to the Druckers' house for Mort to sign. Unfortunately, Drucker forgot to keep a few for himself. Not only did Drucker illustrate the *American Graffiti* poster, he also, of course, drew *MAD's* parody, "American Confetti." Check them both out below.

"Where were you in '62?"—
the *American Graffiti* poster.

MAD #166, April 1974
"American Confetti"

IN CASE YOU MISSED IT

The stormtrooper all the way on the left is not wearing any pants. He's not wearing any skin, either!

SPACE OPERA DEPT.

Once, not too long ago in our galaxy, we were invaded by a movie called "Star Wars" . . . and it was so spectacularly successful that it led to further exploits of "Star Wars" such as posters and dolls and toys and jewelry and coloring books. We feel that it's only a matter of time before we are assaulted by the ultimate "Star Wars" spin-off . . . namely, a musical based on the movie. With this in mind, let's look into the future, as the Editors of MAD present

*What good is watching
some dull, local war,
Night-ly on your TV!
Come to the Gal-ax-y,
my friends!
Come to the Gal-ax-y!

We've got a Death Star
and ray-guns galore—
Kil-ling's improved, you see!
Come to the Gal-ax-y,
my friends!
Come to the Gal-ax-y!

Come see the 'droids!
Come feel the Force!
Come have a blast!
Watch . . . a . . . cru-sad-er
Risk his life
against Darth Vader!

You'll meet a Wookiee
who lets out a roar
Each time we sing off-key!
Come to the Gal-ax-y,
my friends!
Come to the Gal-ax-y!

*Sung to the tune of "Cabaret"

MAD #203, December 1978
"The Force and I: The MAD 'Star Wars' Musical"

FORCE AND I

D "STAR WARS" MUSICAL

ARTIST: MORT DRUCKER   WRITER: FRANK JACOBS

"WORKING FOR THE U.S. POSTAL SERVICE"— ANOTHER VARIANT ON THE R2-D2 MAILBOX GAG

As you have already seen, *MAD* is more than happy to beat an idea into the ground!

*Sung to the tune of "Maria"

THE "OFFICIAL" MUSICAL THAT NEVER GOT OFF THE GROUND

In the early 1990s, Lucasfilm was actually in negotiations with a group of producers who were interested in developing a musical based on *Star Wars*. Unfortunately, the music that was presented to the Lucas team was, in the words of Lucas Licensing president Howard Roffman, "something worthy of a *MAD* parody." The development deal was dropped.

MAILBOXES, ETC.
In the panel immediately to the right is yet *another* mailbox reference!

R2-D2'S BEEPING
R2-D2's "language" is essentially sound designer Ben Burtt recording himself making baby-like beeping sounds and combining them with synthesizer noises. For this, he won an Oscar! You have to wonder how Sir Alec Guinness, who won his Oscar for *The Bridge on the River Kwai* by sweating in a hot jungle, felt about this.

KIRK AND SPOCK
Note the presence of *Star Trek*'s Captain Kirk and Mr. Spock on the left. In 2005, when George Lucas received the American Film Institute's Life Achievement Award, the audience was treated to a surprise musical number from William Shatner. The gag was that Shatner thought he was at a *Star Trek* convention, and then, realizing his error, "improvised" a modified rendition of "My Way" in Lucas's honor, complete with dancing stormtroopers. If you can find it online, you'll see that Harrison Ford thought it was hysterical.

"MY WAY"
Given the rumors that always surrounded Frank Sinatra about his supposed ties to some rather rough mafia figures, having the fearsome Darth Vader of the evil galactic Empire singing a Sinatra tune is a nice touch.

C-3PO AND THE ANSWERING MACHINE

During the period that the original trilogy was being shot on soundstages in the UK, if you were to call the Lucasfilm offices in London and no one was there you actually would have heard C-3PO say the following: "Hello, you have reached the *Star Wars* corporation. I'm afraid Artoo and I are the only ones here. But if you leave your name and number, we will ask a human to return your call. Thank you."

WHY IS LUKE IN THE WRONG SHIP?

Notice that Luke is in a TIE fighter here and not an X-wing. According to Mort Drucker, this was simply done to see if the readers were paying attention. Visual effects supervisor John Knoll reports that ILM also mischievously messed with continuity by putting an X-wing and a TIE fighter into the Coruscant airspeeder chase in Episode II. Of course, as long as ILM was transplanting stuff from the original trilogy into the prequels, you'd think they could have transplanted Princess Leia in her slave girl outfit as well!

Here I am, the **only** pilot left who can de-stroy the Death Star! Help me, Ben . . .

Use the **Force,** Luke!

The Force knows how to find the target, Luke!

The Force knows how to hit the target, Luke!

The Force **also** knows how to cover up, Luke!

What can the Force do, Ben??

What else can the Force do, Ben??

But what if the Force lets me down and misses the target. Ben?

Okay, Artoo! What do we do when we face almost cer-tain death? What **ELSE?!** We sing!!

*We're . . . off to kill the bad guys— And blow them right out of the sky! If we should miss Then you can all kiss Our buddies back there good-bye!

But you can be certain we'll kill the foe By striking the blow That lays them low— Because, because, because, because—I know There's only one way we can end this show!

TWEETLE -BEEP- TWEETLE -DE-BO!

We're off to kill the bad guys— And blow them right out of the sky!

BLAM!

Well, Princess, this is **the end,** right? We did it! We **wiped out** the Death Star and made the Galaxy **safe** for Democracy! Now, we can live happily ever after in **peace and freedom!** Right?

Wrong, Luke! This **CAN'T** be the end! We're going to keep on going, because we **still** have **THE FORCE!!**

*Sung to the tune of "We're Off To See The Wizard"

*We've grown accustomed to the Force That pulls in people to this show! We've grown accustomed to the gross— No other show comes close!

We're big! We're hot! A smash . . . we've got— With tons of money pouring in From fans who make our profits grow!

Although we could have killed Darth Vader, It was not the thing to do! We'll need him in the future when we Bring out "Star Wars II"!

We've grown accustomed to the clout— The way we all made out— Ac-customed to the Force!!

*Sung to the tune of "I've Grown Accustomed To Her Face"

"THE EMPIRE STRIKES BACK"   A DUMB TV SHOW CALLED "QUINCY"   DON MARTIN   DAVE BERG   AL JAFFEE

...and the usual gang of idiots are all in this issue of...

MAD

IND

No. 220 Jan. '81

OUR PRICE 75c CHEAP

CLAW MARKS MADE BY CONSUMERS TRYING TO HOLD DOWN RISING COST OF LIVING

0 70989 33230 0 1

MAD #220, January 1981
Cover, Alfred as Yoda
(Artist: Jack Rickard)

LUCAS SENDS LOVE, HIS LAWYERS SEND LOATHING

When this issue came out, *MAD* received a letter from Lucas's lawyers, demanding that *MAD* cease and desist from using Lucasfilm characters to sell *MAD* Magazine. In addition, they demanded *MAD* turn over all profits made on that issue. Unfortunately for the lawyers, *MAD* had already received a letter from Lucas himself (see page 32), expressing his admiration. As Howard Roffman, current president of Lucas Licensing who was working in the legal department at the time, explains, Lucasfilm legal was in Southern California, while George was in Northern California, and they didn't have much to do with each other. Hence, neither knew what the other had done. Bill Gaines, *MAD*'s publisher, resolved the situation by sending a copy of Lucas's letter to the Southern California lawyers. *MAD* never heard from Lucasfilm legal again.

This is the first version of the Yoda cover by Jack Rickard. When *MAD* asked for minor changes, Rickard decided to start over again from scratch and gave this first attempt to *MAD* staffer Lenny Brenner.
Photo by Brian Durniak. Courtesy of Leonard Brenner.

A modified version of this cover was used for MAD XL #33, June 2005. As you will see, *MAD* likes to recycle the suggestive limp lightsaber gag.

THE MAN IN THE SUNGLASSES

Notice the bearded man wearing the sunglasses in the background on the left. Below we have a photo of George Lucas in his trademark sunglasses. Coincidence? Only Mort Drucker knows for sure.

A 1980s-era photo of George Lucas in his sunglasses.

Speaking of George being in the background, Sid Ganis, the president of the Academy of Motion Picture Arts and Sciences at the time of this writing, was senior vice president of Lucasfilm at the time of *Empire*'s release, and he reports that back then Lucas was rarely recognized by the average man in the street the way he is today. In fact, Ganis recalls an occasion when he, Lucas, and Steven Spielberg were chatting at Lucas's annual Fourth of July picnic at Skywalker Ranch when a young boy came up to the three bearded men and, thinking Ganis was Lucas, asked him for his autograph. When Ganis pointed to Lucas and said, "*He's* actually George Lucas," the boy thought for a moment, looked from Ganis to Lucas and back again, and replied, "No, he's not. *You* are."

The man mistaken for the Jedi Master—Sid Ganis in the early 1980s.
Photo courtesy of Sid Ganis.

MAD #220, January 1981
"Star Bores: The Empire Strikes Out"

STAR
THE **EMPIRE STRIKES OUT** BORES

Arrgg! Arrgg!

Poor Chew-bacco! Is he **crying** because Lube isn't back yet?

No, he's cry-ing because this is the **THIRD** planet we've **been** on that doesn't have **BANANAS** growing on it!

Well, **I'm** going out to **look** for Lube!

With the temperature falling, your Wonton will **freeze** to **death** in 20 minutes!

No, he **won't!** This morning for **breakfast,** instead of his usual **Chicken Soup,** I gave him a bowl of **ANTI-FREEZE!**

SEND THIS BOY TO PLANET OF THE APES

I'm **doomed!** A creature captured me and I'm . . .

Lube . . .

It's **OLDIE VON MOLDIE!!** Oldie . . . what are you doing **UPSIDE-DOWN** . . . ?!?

Lube, you idiot! **YOU'RE** the one who's upside-down!

ARTIST: MORT DRUCKER   **WRITER: DICK DE BARTOLO**

Lube, listen to me! You must go to the **Dairybar System!** There, you will learn from **Yodel,** the **Jet-Eye Master** who taught me!

Sounds great, Oldie! But first, who's going to teach me how to **get down** from **HERE?**

Your lightsaber is nearby! Whatever you **WISH** into your hand shall **BE** in your hand!

Really?? Then **FORGET** about the lightsaber! **I'M** going to wish for a sexy **BLONDE** with a **big pair of scissors!**

Lube! Thank God you're alive! I've brought you some **food!** But first, I must get you **warm!** I'm cutting open my **dead** Wonton and spreading his **intestines** and his **liver** and his **kidneys** all over you! That'll get you warm! Now about the **food—**

Ulp! Choke! Gagg!

Er, Ham . . . **FORGET** about the food! I seem to have **lost** my—ulp—**appetite** for some reason!!

"AN IMPERIAL DRAIDLE!"
You may have noticed *MAD*'s recurring use of variants on the word *draidle* (commonly spelled *dreidel*) both in this parody and in "Star Roars." *Draidle* is a Yiddish word for a kind of top that is played with on the Jewish holiday of Hanukkah. *MAD* has a long history of using Yiddish words because, as writer Dick DeBartolo (an Italian-American) puts it, "Yiddish sounds funny, schmuck!"

I **FOUND** them! I **FOUND** Lube and Ham! And they're both fine, despite that **blistering** storm!

Lube used **The Force** to create some palm trees and sunshine!

How's Lube, Doc? Did being out in that **FRIGID COLD** all night do any damage?

No! But some **idiot** covered him with **animal guts!** THAT did **damage!** But now that he's in the Hydro-Bath, he's no longer suffering from **GUT EXPOSURE!**

Then why does he **LOOK** like he's in pain?!?

Because **NOW** he's suffering from **DROWNING!!! TOO MUCH HYDRO-BATH! STOP THE HYDRO-BATH!** Remove the **RUBBER HYDRO-DUCK!!**

Ham, now that the **emergency** is **over**, why not get on your **90-ton broom** and fly out of here?!

Princess, sometimes I think you **forgot** how to be a woman!

Oh? What makes you say **that**?

Well . . . for openers, you have your **BRA** on backwards!

C'mon, Princess! Stop pretending you **dislike** me! Last night, you showed your **TRUE** feelings for me!

As I recall, last night, I **kicked** you in the **rear thruster!!**

Yeah, but not all that **hard!** If that isn't **love,** what is?!

I'**LL** show you how much I love you, Ham Yoyo!!

That **broad's** got great **lips,** but **lousy eyesight!!**

EREK I'M NOT!

Princess . . . we have a **visitor!**

Tell him we **gave** at the other **planet!**

It's not at the **door!** It's on the **radar screen!** See?

Good Lord!! It's a **stainless steel COCKROACH!** Those things get **more** indestructible each century!

I'm afraid that was an **Imperial Draidle!** Which means they know that we're here!

No! My plan is to remain here, and nothing will upset my plan!!

We have to **vacate** . . .

Oh, yeah?? How about if **I KISS** you . . . ??

That **MAY** upset my **STOMACH** . . . but **not** my plan!!

"YOU INVITED DART ZADER TO DINNER?!"

Notice the skull on the dinner table. No one at *MAD* is exactly sure what the entrée was (nor, for that matter, how the fearsome Sith Lord managed to eat or drink through his mask), but perhaps some questions are better left unanswered.

TOO MANY HANS

Note that Han appears *after* he has been frozen in carbonite (far left). *MAD* got some grief for this not only from the fans, but from Lucas himself, as can be seen in the letter on the next page. In the letter Lucas asks if, since *MAD* has freed Han from the carbon freeze, he can skip making the next movie. *MAD* was grateful he didn't, as *Return of the Jedi* helped sell a hell of a lot of magazines.

CAN GEORGE LUCAS TIME TRAVEL?

You might have noticed that this letter from George Lucas is dated November 25, 1980, yet it refers to *MAD*'s *Empire* parody, which was in an issue cover-dated January 1981. You are, therefore, probably wondering how Lucas saw an issue from the future. This is because, as mentioned earlier in the book, *MAD* used to come out only eight times a year, and it was common for issues to hit the stands three months in advance of their cover date. Thus, it is not so strange that Lucas saw a January 1981 issue in the fall of 1980. So, no, George Lucas cannot time travel (although ILM is probably working on it).

GEORGE LUCAS
San Anselmo, California

November 25, 1980

Mad Magazine
Department 220
485 Madison Avenue
New York, New York 10022

Attention: Mr. John Ficcara

Dear Mad:

I think that special Oscars should be awarded to Mort Drucker and Dick DeBartolo - the George Bernard Shaw and Leonardo DiVinci of comic satire.

Their sequel to my sequel was sheer galactic madness.

I especially enjoyed their facility in getting Han Solo out of carbon freeze in time to pilot the Millennium to freedom. Does this mean that I can skip Episode VI?

Keep up the good Farce!

Sincerely,

George W. Lucas

GWL:law

George Lucas's Letter to *MAD* in Admiration of
"Star Bores: The Empire Strikes Out", November 25, 1980

A SEQUEL OPPORTUNITY EMPLOYER DEPT.

Most everyone who's seen *"Star Wars"* and *"The Empire Strikes Back"* is wondering what George Lucas is planning for his *next* sequel! We've heard he's planning a total of nine films, or is it eight, or twelve? There are reports the first two films aren't *really* the first chronologically, that they fall somewhere in the *middle!* And what about Luke Skywalker? Is he the son of Darth Vader? Will he marry Princess Leia? What's ahead for Han Solo and Artoo-Detoo? Well, we at MAD figure *someone's* got to have a master plan of the whole mess, right? *Right!* And what does that carefully guarded master plan look like? *Heh heh...*

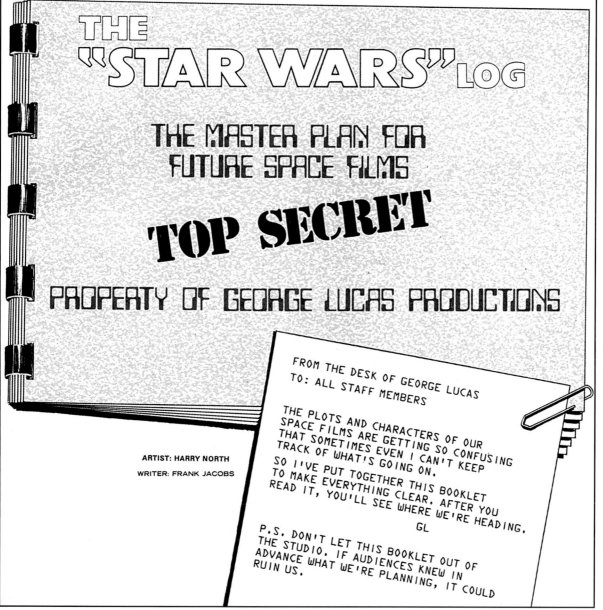

THE **"STAR WARS"** LOG

THE MASTER PLAN FOR FUTURE SPACE FILMS

TOP SECRET

PROPERTY OF GEORGE LUCAS PRODUCTIONS

ARTIST: HARRY NORTH
WRITER: FRANK JACOBS

FROM THE DESK OF GEORGE LUCAS
TO: ALL STAFF MEMBERS

THE PLOTS AND CHARACTERS OF OUR SPACE FILMS ARE GETTING SO CONFUSING THAT SOMETIMES EVEN I CAN'T KEEP TRACK OF WHAT'S GOING ON. SO I'VE PUT TOGETHER THIS BOOKLET TO MAKE EVERYTHING CLEAR. AFTER YOU READ IT, YOU'LL SEE WHERE WE'RE HEADING.
GL

P.S. DON'T LET THIS BOOKLET OUT OF THE STUDIO. IF AUDIENCES KNEW IN ADVANCE WHAT WE'RE PLANNING, IT COULD RUIN US.

MAD #230, April 1982
"The 'Star Wars' Log"

Altogether, there will be 12 films in our epic space saga, but they will not be made in chronological order. "Star Wars" and "The Empire Strikes Back," our first two films, are actually No. 5 and No. 6 in the series.

Our third picture (really No. 2 in the series) will be "Send in the Clones," in which we find out that both Darth Vader and Obi-Wan Kenobi were cloned by the same donor, who happens to be a long-lost grandfather of Chewbacca's. This sets up a conflict between the Wookies and the Empire, which becomes the plot for our fourth film (No. 3 in the series), "Makin' Wookie."

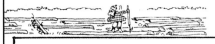

Meanwhile, in our sixth film, "Hiya, Leia" (No. 10 in the series), Princess Leia discovers that her grandfather and Han Solo's grandmother were next-door neighbors on Alderaan, before it was blown up by Darth Vader (in "Star Wars"). In a wild, galactic battle, Luke fights Boba Fett, and we are left with the impression that Boba may be Luke's father.

After seeing "The Empire Strikes Back," some people got the idea that Darth Vader is Luke Skywalker's real father. Although "Makin' Wookie" doesn't clear this up, it does reveal how an ancestor of Princess Leia befriends Yoda, who organizes the Jedi Knights, comprised of Darth Vader (then a young idealist in love with Lando Calrissian's great-aunt) and Obi-Wan Kenobi, who defend the Wookies when their home, the planet Kazhyyyk, is overrun by droids (film No. 11, "Cut and Droid").

This ties in neatly with our fifth film (No. 1 in the series), "A Matter of Life and Darth," in which Luke, who has unraveled the secrets of time travel (in "Makin' Wookie"), learns that Darth Vader is a half-droid and may be the father of both Han Solo and See-Threepio. Luke gets this information from Yoda, who reveals that Darth Vader, being part droid, distrusts humans and plans to organize all the droids in the hope of destroying the Rebel Alliance.

This brings us to our seventh film, "Cut and Droid" (No. 11 in the series), which recounts the Great Droid War, in which See-Threepio apparently dies, after a valiant battle against rust. This should not be confused with the plot of our eighth film, "Look, Ma, No Han" (No. 9 in the series), in which Han Solo is forced to become an undercover agent for Darth Vader, and is lost in hyper-space after Artoo-Detoo reveals that Princess Leia may be the daughter of Obi-Wan Kenobi from his first marriage to a sister of Boba Fett's great-grandmother.

THE "GREAT DROID WAR"

Here, way back in 1982, MAD's Frank Jacobs anticipates a Great Droid War—which is, of course, essentially what is going on in the prequel trilogy: a war between droids and clones. Jacobs turned out to be way off base, however, in predicting Obi-Wan's marital history.

The battle droids ready for war.

Both Boba Fett and Jabba the Hut (who are introduced in "The Empire Strikes Back") were once comrades of Darth Vader, and this is brought out in our ninth film, "Yessir, That's My Boba" (No. 4 in the series). We find out that Luke Skywalker's lightsaber was once recharged by Boba Fett's father, who we suspect may be Chewbacca. This ties in with the romance between See-Threepio (who learns he is part-human) and Chewbacca's half-hairy sister, Varga (introduced in "Cut and Droid").

Here we learn from Artoo-Detoo (who holds the entire history of the Galaxy in his memory banks) how the Jedi Knights were disbanded, and also observe See-Threepio's nervous breakdown, when he finds out that mixed marriages sometimes don't work.

We learn more about Luke's ancestry in our eleventh film, "Space 'n Vader" (No. 7 in the series) as the Jedi Knights split into three factions—one loyal to Princess Leia, another loyal to Darth Vader, and a third having no opinion. Luke returns from a

space voyage to the planet Kazhyyyk where he discovers the true identity of his father while rescuing Chewbacca from midget aliens. Luke, as it turns out, lived as a young boy with the Wookies, who snatched him from a drone spaceship just outside the Mandalore System, the home of Boba Fett and other Super Commandos. The Wookies gave Luke the name of "Skywalker," which, in the Wookie tongue, means "Hairless Warrior Who Destroys Evil With Beam of Light." Now Luke learns from Artoo-Detoo that neither Darth Vader, Obi-Wan Kenobi, nor Boba Fett is his father.

However, we always come back to the question of who is Luke's father, and in our tenth film, "Lando Plenty" (No. 8 in the series), we discover that Lando Calrissian's great-aunt (whom we met in "Makin' Wookie") may have been the wife of Obi-Too Kenobi (Obi-Wan's younger brother) in Cloud City, when Lando's father joined forces with a cousin of Han Solo's to put down the First Droid Uprising, which leads to the Great Droid War (seen in "Cut and Droid").

In our twelfth film, "Once a Knight Is Enough" (No. 12 in the series), the identity of Luke's father is finally revealed. It is none other than The Force, which, as we learned in "Send in the Clones," was once capable of taking on human form before it dissolved into the Sixth Dimension. Luke is reunited with Princess Leia (who has left Darth Vader after being forced to marry him in "Hiya, Leia") and they move to another galaxy.

This last film serves as the climax to the "Star Wars Saga—Part I." Immediately after it is completed (we figure that to be sometime around the year 2014), we will begin work on the 24 films that make up the "Star Wars Saga—Part II."

"LUKE'S FATHER IS...NONE OTHER THAN THE FORCE"
Finally, in perhaps the strongest testament to Frank Jacobs's powers of precognition, we are presented with a scenario in which the Force is Luke Skywalker's father. This is eerily reminiscent of the "virgin birth" from Episode I, in which the midi-chlorians—biological carriers of the Force—impregnated Anakin's mother, Shmi Skywalker. Frank, maybe it's time you cashed in and started a psychic hotline!

ODD, RANDOM USELESS FACTS

Artist Monte Wolverton reports that he clearly recalls "having a craving for cinnamon rolls and sausage (bratwurst, I think) after working on this piece."

On an unrelated note, Wolverton is also president of the Rat Terrier Club of America at the time of this writing.

MAD Star Wars Spectacular, 1996
"One Fine Day in a Galaxy Far, Far Away"

MAD

No. 242
Oct. '83

IND

OUR PRICE
$1.00
CHEAP

UNMASKS "THE RETURN OF THE JEDI" AND "THE A-TEAM"

CROSS SECTION OF MR. T'S
MOHAWK HAIRCUT TODAY...

AND AS
A BABY

10

0

70989 33230

RICHARD
WILLIAMS

VIOLATING "THE FICARRA DOCTRINE"

This cover violates what later at *MAD* came to be known as "the Ficarra Doctrine," named after current *MAD* chief John Ficarra. The doctrine dictates that two pop-culture properties should never be merged into the same cover gag, as they will usually devolve into a confusing, amalgamated abomination. Al Feldstein, who was editor-in-chief at the time this cover was created, agrees, and asserts that mixing *Return of the Jedi* and *The A-Team* was one of his few regrets from his tenure at *MAD*. Years later, however, Feldstein was somewhat vindicated when Conan O'Brien trotted out an "R2-Mr.T2" droid in May of 2007, when George Lucas was a guest on his show, demonstrating that maybe there was indeed something funny to be found in the fusing of the two icons.

Conan O'Brien's R2-Mr.T2.
Photo by Stacey Leong.
© Lucasfilm Ltd. & TM. All rights reserved.

MAD #242, October 1983
Cover, Mr. T as Darth Vader and Alfred as Wicket
(Artist: Richard Williams)

THE FARCE BE WITH YOU DEPT.

Hi! I'm **Princess Laidup!** Note that I'm wearing **less clothes** in this movie than before! That's 'cause my **Figure's improved!** Unfortunately, my **acting HASN'T!**

I'm **Ham Yoyo!** And this is my good friend, **Chewbacco!**

Arg! Arg! Arrrgghh!

But it **does** make me jealous that he gets the **best lines** in the movie!!

Hello! I am **Dart Zader!** My big kick in life is to **threaten** and **scare** people! I got my training working for the **I.R.S.!**

I'm **Landough!** I'm **proud** to be in a movie that gives work to **minorities!** No, I'm **not talking** about **Blacks!** I'm talking about **Ewoks, Chirpas, Jubbas** and **Freens!**

I'm **Cree-pio!** I think I've **had** it after this movie… unless they want me as **The Tin Man** in a remake of **"The Wizard of Oz"!**

I'm **Lube Skystalker!** In this movie, **I find** out who **my Father** is…!

And **after** this movie, I sure hope your **REAL Father** has a good **business** you can go into!!

I'm **Bar-Stool!** I've already had an **offer** that'll keep me busy **24** hours a day! I'm going to be a garbage can!

MAY THE DWARFS BE WITH YOU

"I'M GOING TO BE A GARBAGE CAN!"
As you have no doubt noticed by now, like the R2-D2-as-mailbox gag, *MAD* also likes "recycling" the R2-D2-as-trash-can gag. You'll see it again before this book is over.

MAD #242, October 1983
"Star Bores: Re-hash of the Jeti"

STAR BORES

RE-HASH OF THE JETI

ARTIST: MORT DRUCKER   WRITER: DICK DE BARTOLO

"MAY THE HORSE BE WITH YOU"

After Mort Drucker drew his pencils, longtime *MAD* editor Nick Meglin did his usual thing—going through the art and inserting numerous horrible (by Meglin's own admission) puns on "May the Force Be with You" to make the parody that much more *MAD*. We count nine variations on the pun in this spoof.

Horses actually do play an odd role in the *Star Wars* universe. A character named Hohass (Runt) Ekwesh is an X-wing pilot introduced in the novel *X-wing: Wraith Squadron*. An illustration of him appears in *Star Wars: The New Essential Guide to Characters*. As die-hard *Star Wars* fans know from *The Making of Star Wars: Revenge of the Sith*, the Episode III art department thought this character was absolutely hysterical and adopted him as their mascot, even going so far as to design a modified X-wing for him.

Hohass (Runt) Ekwesh as seen in *Star Wars: The New Essential Guide to Characters*.
Illustration by Michael Sutfin.
© Lucasfilm Ltd. & TM. All rights reserved.

Ekwesh's modified X-wing, designed by Episode III art department member Alex Jaeger.
Images courtesy of Warren Fu.
© Lucasfilm Ltd. & TM. All rights reserved.

"GLITCH!"
Note the "glitch" sound effect in the far right panel. To most people, "glitch" is a problem with their computer, but all *MAD* readers know that "glitch" is a popular *MAD* sound effect for stepping in fecal matter.

Al Jaffee's classic renderings of the sound of stepping in "doggie-do" from "*MAD* Solutions to Big City Doggie-Do Problems," *MAD* #172, January 1975.

"ENGLISH PERFECT?!?"

Frank Oz explains that the reason Yoda speaks the way he does is because that's the way Jedi spoke hundreds of years ago and Yoda is keeping the old way of speaking alive. It's as if someone who grew up in Shakespeare's time were still alive today and still spoketh Shakespearean English. *MAD*, however, still goes with the 900-years-old-and-senile theory.

"**OKAY, AUDIENCE...ALL TOGETHER NOW!!**"
Dick DeBartolo's observation that the Rebel Alliance was using the same plan they used before, and, on top of that, driving the point home by having Admiral Ackbar ask the audience to recite it, is up there with some of *MAD*'s finer moments.

"**BRING US A STACK OF BUCKWHEATS!**"
Once again, *MAD* poses the question Lucasfilm doesn't want asked: How *does* Darth Vader eat through that mask?

"NO, LUBE, THAT'S BECAUSE OF MY BAD EYESIGHT!"

MAD wasn't far off the mark with this joke. The stormtrooper and Vader masks are notorious for being difficult to see out of. In fact, according to Lorne Peterson, there is an outtake from the scene in the original *Star Wars* where Vader and the stormtroopers are supposed to dramatically board Princess Leia's ship—but instead one of the stormtroopers trips, causing a bunch of them to fall over like dominoes and making Vader himself stumble.

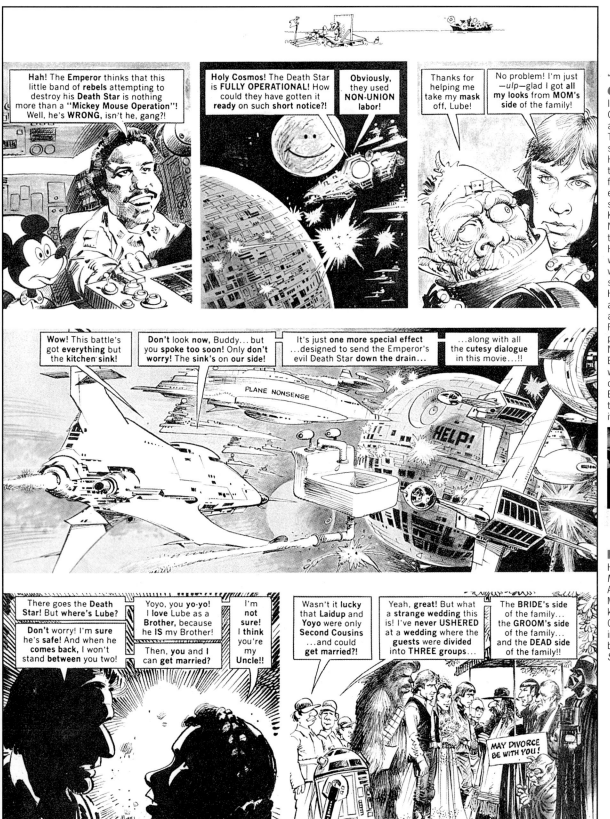

"MICKEY MOUSE OPERATION"

In *Return of the Jedi*, Lando Calrissian's copilot is actually a little alien named Nien Nunb. To give him an alien language, sound designer Ben Burtt used Haya, an African language, thinking it would be too obscure for anyone to recognize. He enlisted a Kenyan student studying in California named Kipsang Rotich to read Nien Nunb's lines and figured that would be the end of it. However, *Return of the Jedi* was actually shown in Kenya, where audiences were both shocked and thrilled to hear Haya coming from the little alien's mouth. Shortly thereafter, Nien Nunb and Kipsang Rotich were a national phenomenon! As for what Nien Nunb was actually saying, Burtt reports that the attempt was made to have the meaning of his Haya lines match the English subtitling, but only the Kenyans know for sure if it actually did.

Nien Nunb and Lando Calrissian.

KITCHEN SINK

Here is another example of *MAD* beating ILM to the punch. Almost twenty years after Mort Drucker threw in a kitchen sink, ILM did the same. One of the pieces of debris in the space battle at the beginning of *Revenge of the Sith* is, in fact, a kitchen sink.

CLIP SERVICE DEPT. PART II

DON MARTIN'S

RETURN OF THE JEDI

NO STAR WARS TOASTERS OR RUGS
Lucasfilm director of content management and fan relations, and *Star Wars* collector extraordinaire, Steve Sansweet tells us that there never were any *Star Wars* toasters or Ewok rugs. So if there are any licensees out there reading this, here's a couple of opportunities for ya!

Oh, Han! These little **Ewoks** are so **cute**... and **soft**...!

You're right!

MAD #243, December 1983
"Don Martin's 'Return of the Jedi' Out-takes"

OUT–TAKES

PLUGGING IN THE LIGHTSABER

In the 1989 Hong Kong film *Pedicab Driver*, actor-director Sammo Hung (perhaps best known in America for the TV series *Martial Law,* in which he was teamed with Arsenio Hall and Kelly Hu) pays comedic tribute to *Star Wars* by doing something similar to this Martin gag—a "lightsaber" battle in which the combatants fight with fluorescent lightbulbs.

WHAT SAFE, CHEAP "STAR WARS" TECHNOLOGY WOULD WE LIKE TO SUGGEST TO THE PENTAGON?

HERE WE GO WITH ANOTHER RIDICULOUS
MAD FOLD-IN

Everyone's arguing about the merits of "Star Wars" space weapons. To find out what the only intelligent solution really is, fold page in as shown in diagram at the right.

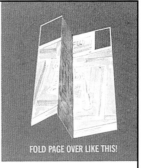

FOLD PAGE OVER LIKE THIS!

A ► FOLD BACK SO "A" MEETS "B" ◄ B

REAGAN AND STAR WARS

Back in the 1980s, Ronald Reagan proposed something called the Strategic Defense Initiative (SDI). The idea was to have a space-based anti-missile system defending America from the Soviets. It was nicknamed "Star Wars" by the Democrats—a moniker subsequently picked up by the popular press, which didn't exactly fill Lucasfilm with joy. According to Lucas Licensing president Howard Roffman, while Lucasfilm couldn't stop the public from using the nickname, it did use legal means to try to stop two private organizations from using it in television spots. While Lucasfilm did not win the case, the court decision did reaffirm Lucasfilm's right to defend its trademark. "The Usual Gang of Idiots," meanwhile, had its own issues with Cold War-era nicknames, given that the doctrine of Mutually Assured Destruction was frequently referred to as "MAD." As for *MAD*'s opinion about the "Star Wars" defense system, in addition to the sentiments expressed by this Fold-in, *MAD* senior editor Charlie Kadau penned this Alfred E. Neuman quote in *MAD* #259, December 1985: "The biggest flaw in the 'Star Wars' system is that it will drive the Soviets to develop an 'Empire Strikes Back' system!"

NO NEED TO RUIN YOUR BOOK BY FOLDING THIS PAGE! JUST TURN TO THE NEXT PAGE TO SEE THE ANSWER!

ARTIST & WRITER:
AL JAFFEE

REAGAN ADMINISTRATION MILITARY PLANNERS WANT THEIR SCIENTISTS TO CREATE WEAPONS IN SPACE TO DESTROY ENEMY MISSILES OVER OUR LANDSCAPE

A ► ◄ B

MAD #256, July 1985
Fold-in, "What Safe, Cheap 'Star Wars' Technology Would We Like to Suggest to the Pentagon?"

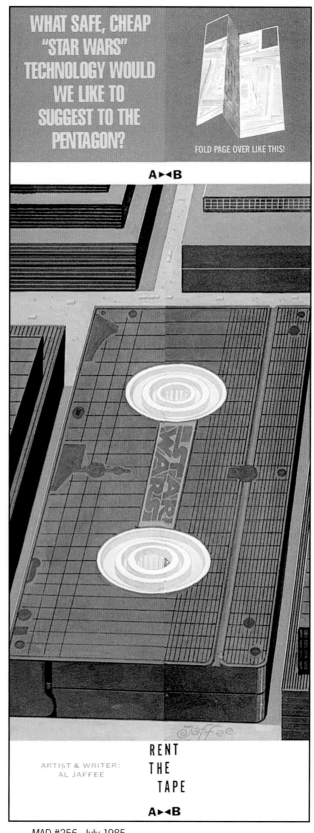

MAD #256, July 1985
Fold-in FOLDED!

When a filmmaker like George Lucas sets out to create a work that will bear his name, he has but one lofty goal, one higher plane he hopes to reach — making money! And lots of it! It's no surprise that a businessman like ol' George figured out that as good as his three *Star Wars* flicks were, the real dough is in the toys! So he licensed playsets and action figures that hop off the shelf faster than you can say "Mommy, I wanna Wookie." But for every successful Millennium Falcon or Death Star toy, there were the lesser-knowns, the also-rans, the unwanted merchandising items like these...

STAR WARS PLAYSETS

YOU MAY HAVE MISSED

ARTIST: JAMES WARHOLA   WRITER: DAVID SHAYNE

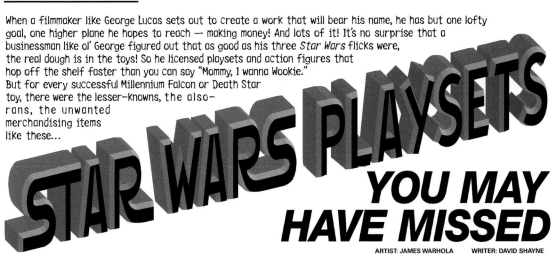

STAR WARS: THE FINAL FRONTIER

At first blush, it seemed like a good idea: combine the two most popular science fiction franchises in motion picture history — *Star Wars* and *Star Trek* — to create the ultimate toy spaceship, the Millennium Enterprise. But bringing these two unrelated universes together only confused and frustrated kids! Who commands the ship, they asked, Luke or Kirk? Is that load of blubber in Sick Bay Jabba the Hutt or Scotty? Is that Kirk's real hair, or is Chewbacca shedding again? Who knows? Who cares? Certainly not the toy-buying public, which avoided this plastic monstrosity like a lice-infested Ewok!

MORE SIX DEGREES OF *STAR WARS*/ *MAD* SEPARATION

Hayden Christensen played Anakin Skywalker. He was also in *Factory Girl*, which was about Andy Warhol hanger-on Edie Sedgwick. Andy Warhol's nephew, James Warhola, illustrated this article. Looks like Luke Skywalker isn't the only one related to everyone in the galaxy!

MAD #354, February 1997
"*Star Wars* Playsets You May Have Missed"

THE STRANGEST REAL-WORLD *STAR WARS* PRODUCT

One common complaint of *MAD* writers is, "How do you top a world gone mad?" Case in point: the Jar Jar "Monster Mouth" candy. According to Howard Roffman, president of Lucas Licensing, the Jar Jar candy is perhaps the *Star Wars* brand's strangest licensed product. It was essentially Jar Jar's head with a syringe-like mechanism at the base. When the "syringe's" plunger was pushed in, Jar Jar's plastic mouth would open wide, and a large piece of candy in the shape of Jar Jar's tongue would come out—seemingly encouraging children to suck on a Gungan tongue. If that weren't bad enough, there was a spate of Internet humor claiming that evangelical Christians were condemning the "Monster Mouth" as some sort of sexual device. In the words of C-3PO, "Oh my!"

The infamous Jar Jar "Monster Mouth" candy.
Photo by Anne Neumann. © Lucasfilm Ltd. & TM. All rights reserved.

THE DIZZY DROID DRAG CANTINA

Saving the galaxy ain't exactly a spacewalk in the park — just ask Luke Skywalker! Between getting his hand cut off (by his own father no less) and finding out that the woman he loves is his sister, Luke has a couple of emotional skeletons in his closet that he needs to let out from time to time. So where does a frustrated Jedi Knight head to cut loose? To the Dizzy Droid, the Empire's only "alternative" watering hole. At this intergalactic drag bar, Luke can put away his drab pilot duds, throw on his best Versace floor-length Wookie fur coat, and have a drink with other "space" explorers! Based on a *Star Wars* scene left on the cutting room floor, this playset includes four bonus figures: the Extraterrestrial Village People.

LA DIZZY DROID

AL'S IMPERIAL JIFFY LUBE AND GARAGE

Meet Al Mertzer, Mechanic to the Empire. This poor action figure has the unenviable task of doing all the unpleasant-but-necessary dirty work that keeps a galaxy running! From scraping the corpses of Rebel pilots off the feet of an Imperial AT-AT Walker to cleaning up TIE Fighters whose pilots couldn't quite stomach the jump to Hyperspace, Al's done it all at his garage. Playset features a working turbo lift, lube station and landspeeder bay. Deluxe set also includes three action figures: Al, Hank-G48 and Fred-bot, Al's two drunken assistant mechanics, with real cursing action!

CHEWBACCA'S INTERGALACTIC FUR HUT

The au courant Wookie or Ewok in search of a hip, new image need look no further than this trendy salon in the heart of the Empire's fashion district. From Milan to Alderaan, Chewie's head stylist Tonytron (known to his friends as the Jedi Master of Haircuts) travels the galaxy to hire haircutters who know the latest in body-hair braiding and mane styling. French Poodle cuts, David Schwimmer-style Caesars or Tonytron's special, the Grand Coif Tarkin — they're all available at Chewbacca's Intergalactic Fur Hut! Combination lightsaber/hair clippers not included.

YODA'S SWINGIN' PAD

Sure, in *The Empire Strikes Back,* Yoda lived in a dingy swamp, but when he isn't training Luke how to kick some stormtrooper ass, Yoda likes to chill somewhere a little more chic than a slimy, bug-infested mudhole. And that somewhere is Yoda's Swingin' Pad, the kind of laid-back bachelor apartment where a three-foot, 900-year-old muppet can entertain the ladies in style. With Yoda's Swingin' Pad, kids will learn how to woo the babes — and they'll love playing with Yoda's margarita mixer, mirrored bed and an actual, working condom machine! As the Jedi Master himself says, "A special way I have with the ladies!"

JABBA THE HUTT'S BATHROOM

After sitting around all day eating that greasy Tattooine food, where in the palace does Jabba go to ease his 30' colon? The "throne room," of course! Technicians from Industrial Light and Magic spent months digitizing the seven realistic bathroom noises this playset makes, such as the sound of Jabba after he's had a little too much bran. Set includes intergalactic toilet with real Hyperspace flusher! Stormtrooper Washroom Attendant and Janitor figures with gas masks sold separately.

TRIPPING THE IMPERIAL WALKER

According to ILM veteran Lorne Peterson, the first take of Luke Skywalker causing the menacing Imperial walker to collapse was unusable because the machine fell slowly backward onto its back legs like a scared little puppy. Not exactly the dramatic effect they were going for.

MAD #354, February 1997
Back Cover, "One Day on the Snowy Plains of Hoth"
(Writer: Duck Edwing; Artist: Paul Coker)

MAD #354, February 1997
Cover, Alfred as Jabba the Hutt
(Artist: Richard Williams)

TRYING TO RECAPTURE THAT OLD INDUSTRIAL LIGHT AND MAGIC DEPT.

Next spring, George Lucas is releasing a version of his *Star Wars* trilogy that boasts computer-enhanced graphics, digitally re-mastered sound and never-before-seen clips from all three movies! In other words, he's going to make the lightsabers orange instead of red, turn up the bass on the soundtrack and add three minutes of scenes that should have stayed on the cutting room floor! Too bad, because Lucas had a golden opportunity to make the *Star Wars* trilogy much more *au courant!* Instead of sitting at his ranch counting up the profits from action figure sales, maybe our buddy George could have taken our suggestions for...

UPDATING STAR WARS FOR THE FUTURE

MAD'S IDEAS WEREN'T AS SURPRISING AS THE REALITY

As extreme as *MAD*'s ideas for updating *Star Wars* might have seemed, they were nowhere near as surprising as the "Jedi Rocks" musical number inserted into *Return of the Jedi*, or, of course, the infamous "Greedo Shoots First" edit in *A New Hope*.

Help me, Obi-Wan — you're my **only hope!** I'm so **hot** and it's so **lonely** on this **battlecruiser!** I need you and your **big, mighty lightsaber!**

Have Luke Skywalker use R2-D2 to gain access to cyber-porn!

I love you, man!

Instead of "May the Force Be With You," change the Star Wars slogan to something a little more contemporary!

Have Chewbacca shave his body hair, get a tattoo, pierce his nose and move to the East Village!

MAD #354, February 1997
"Updating *Star Wars* for the Future"

MAY THE FORCE BEAT WITH YOU DEPT.

Hola, los readers! I'm Señor George Lucas, creator of the legendary *Star Wars* movies! This year is the trilogy's 20th anniversary, and I'm cashing in el big-time-o by introducing Luke and the gang to a whole new generation of los gullible fans! And what better way to do it than to ride on the jalapeno-hot coattails of the most popular dance since The Lambada (the forbidden dance of love)! So, grab hold of your lightsaber and feel the Force, as we sing the...

Obi-Wan Kenobi, he get by
on Jedi pension!
He now suffer from arthritis –
constipation not to mention!
Try to use El Force-o, brain
all dried up like adobe!
HEY, BEN KENOBI!

Flyboy is Han Solo, hot to
jump on Princess Leia!
But Leia, she play hardball,
never give him time of day-a!
Han no give a damn – soon
Indy Jones his primo role-o!
HEY, FLYBOY SOLO!

Dark Side turn Darth Vader
into deep-space Dr. Death-o!
He turn off Rebels plenty
with his wheezy morning breath-o!
Whole planets he wipe out –
no one to stop him like Ralph Nader!
HEY, EL LORD VADER!

Wookie El Chewbacca show off
shaggy Bigfoot torso!
He member of El Hair Club —
La Rogaine he now endorso!
Han Solo, he comprende
— Wookie lingo mucho screwy!
HEY, SEÑOR CHEWY!

Bimbo Princess Leia she play
hard to get, by golly!
When she strip down to her skivvies,
she one very hot tamale!
Mucho kicks she gets when men
they bow down, and obey-a!
HEY, PRINCESS LEIA!

I THINK WE'RE DOING THE LAMBADA.

MAD #354, February 1997
"*Star Wars* Macarena"

STAR WARS AND AN EARLIER FAD
Years before the Macarena, disco versions of John Williams's *Star Wars* themes were recorded by Meco and became huge hits. This, of course, was back when music was recorded on a substance called "vinyl." (Ask your grandparents about it.)

Meco's *Star Wars* disco album.
Photo by Anne Neumann. Courtesy of the Steve Sansweet collection.

THAT WEIRD "AJ" THING DANCING IN FRONT OF JABBA
"AJ" is Mort Drucker's grandson Alex Julian. The Gamorrean guard dancing next to him is no relation.

TAR WARS ACARENA

Jedi maestro Yoda he
        no bigger than a taco!
Come across like drop-out Muppet –
        ears he steal from Mr. Spock-o!
Lives on distant planet –
        no one sure of his Zip Code-a!
        HEY, MAESTRO YODA!

Luke-o all shook up when
        learn Darth Vader is his padre!
Find out Leia she his sister –
        hope that Jabba not his madre!
Mucho stupefied like gringo
        bombed out on Sambucco!
        HEY, SEÑOR LUKE-O!

Robot Artoo-Deetoo he
        computer mucho grande!
So smart that even
        Windows 95 he understand!
Glad to show you cyber-porn
        once price you both agree to!
        HEY, ARTOO-DEETO!

Jabba fat like Limbaugh –
        grande glutton roly-poly!
He pig out on compadres –
        make them instant guacamole!
Soon el groundo shake-o
        with a belcho furioso!
        HEY, JABBA GROSSO!

Gabby droid See-Threepio
        he big pain in el but-to!
All the time he fuss and worry –
        his big mouth he never shut-o!
Other droids they think
        a closet gay he just might be-o!
        HEY, SEE-THREEPIO!

Viva Star Wars movies and
        el megabucks they gross-o!
Viva merchandising!
        Viva profits tremendoso!
Viva dolls and comic books
        and T-shirts we supplying!
        HEY, KEEP ON BUYING!

ARTIST: MORT DRUCKER   WRITER: FRANK JACOBS

DANCING STORMTROOPERS

If you really want to see dancing stormtroopers, Anthony Daniels (C-3PO) recommends you try tracking down the 1977 *Star Wars*-themed episode of *Donny & Marie*—an exercise in the bizarre that starred Donny as Luke, Marie as Leia (Lucasfilm's lawyers assure us that George didn't get the Luke/Leia sibling idea from this), Redd Foxx as Obi-Wan, Kris Kristofferson as Han Solo, Paul Lynde as Grand Moff Tarkin, Daniels as C-3PO, Peter Mayhew as Chewbacca, and R2-D2 as himself.

In case you are wondering who was behind this, not only was the writing supervised by longtime *MAD* writer Arnie Kogen (who was also one of the show's producers), but one of the credited writers was none other than Bruce Vilanch, who, you will recall, was also partly to blame for the "*Star Wars* Holiday Special"!

Donny & Marie's dancing stormtroopers.

R2-D2 GETS AROUND

Note R2-D2 falling in love with the coffeemaker on the far right. Is he two-timing the fire hydrant from *Sesame Street*? And what about the mailbox from "A *MAD* Look at 'Star Wars'"? Well, according to Anthony Daniels (C-3PO), R2-D2 *is* a total slut.

MAD Star Wars Spectacular, 1996
"A *MAD* Peek Behind the Scenes at the Making of the *Star Wars* Trilogy"

the Making of the STAR WARS TriLogy

WRITER: DICK DEBARTOLO

Speech bubbles:

Gosh, those **actors** playing the **Imperial Stormtroopers** are **really scary**! They're even scary off **camera**!

They're **not** actors! They're moonlighting **postal workers**! And we saved a **fortune** by **hiring** them! They're **using** their **own weapons**!

The guy **playing** Chewbacca eats **dog food** for **lunch**?

He **says** he **wants** to **stay** in character!

I **hope** those guys like the **look** of the Ewoks that I **designed**!

Are they **executives** from the **movie studio**?

No, they're **executives** from **Toys R Us**! If they don't **think** they'll make a **hot seller**, they **don't** get **into** the **movie**!

MOONLIGHTING STORMTROOPERS

Lucasfilm has a history of using less-than-competent stormtroopers. I, myself, am one such example. When filming some added scenes for the Special Edition of *The Empire Strikes Back*, I was given the chance to be a stormtrooper. Unfortunately, once I put the armor on, it was clear that I was too skinny to be a storm-trooper—the armor kept clattering off me. To keep it on I had to raise my arms zombie-like and shake my hips in a rather girlish manner. To say I was an embarrassment to the Empire would be an understatement. Luckily, the shot ended up being a long shot, and very, very quick, so I am hardly noticeable.

Here I am as a bashful stormtrooper with gigantic glasses.
Photo by Halina Krukowski.

CHEWBACCA EATING DOG FOOD

Peter Mayhew, aka Chewbacca, has suggested that were Chewbacca to indeed endorse a dog food, it would have to be some sort of Lucasfilm-licensed "Chowbacca" brand. *MAD* wonders if dogs would find it too…chewy? (*MAD* also apologizes for the awful pun.)

February 11, 1997

Ms. Amy Vozeolas
MAD Magazine
1700 Broadway
New York, New York 10019

Dear Amy:

Thanks so much for sending the issue of MAD that features the "Star Wars" articles. I can't wait to get home to read it!

Sincerely,

George Lucas

GWL/am

P.O. Box 2009, San Rafael, California 94912-2009   Telephone (415) 662-1800

Thank-you Note from George Lucas, February 11, 1997

1 MONICAGATE
THE NEVER-ENDING SAGA

Sinister villains, classic confrontations, hideous creatures, and yes, even a princess — albeit one with a thonged butt the size of Nebraska. The White House scandal had all the elements of a sci-fi epic, except one — there were no heroes.

ARTIST: MARK STUTZMAN

STARR WARS

Not so long ago, in a country not so far away...

It is a period of civil lawsuits. A horny President, investigated by a relentless Special Prosecutor, claims, "I did not have sex with that woman, Miss Lewinksy."

During the tumultuous legal battle, the evil Special Prosecutor managed to obtain lurid testimony from Miss Lewinsky about the Commander-In-Chief's dark side and THE DEATH CIGAR, a bizarre sexual prop with enough power to destroy an entire Presidency.

Pursued by an ever-vigilant Republican Congress, the embattled President desperately hides behind his lawyers, custodians of the flimsy defense that he hopes can save his political ass...

MAD #377, January 1999
"Starr Wars"

SLICK WILLIE SKYWALKER

This poster parody was created for *MAD*'s "20 Dumbest People, Events & Things of 1998." It became so popular all over the world that, in a bizarre twist, it was made into a series of stamps in the formerly Soviet Abkhazia. *MAD*'s lawyers considered suing, but they gave up on the idea when they realized they would have needed heavily armed NATO troops to serve the papers.

The Abkhazian
"Starr Wars" stamps.

WHAT'S WITH USING THE *STAR WARS* CHARACTERS AS LETTERS?

MAD has a tradition of creating "tribute books" as gifts for members of the *MAD* "family." Each member of "the Usual Gang of Idiots" writes and/or draws something funny for the recipient, and it is all assembled into a big book. *MAD* editor-in-chief John Ficarra remembered that way back in 1982, Mort Drucker had done a nice job of using characters and objects to spell out veteran editor Nick Meglin's name when the staff was giving Meglin a tribute book, and asked him to do something similar for this cover.

Mort Drucker's contribution to the Nick Meglin tribute book.
Courtesy of Nick Meglin.

THE PHANTOM MENACE: *WE HAVE THE MISSING DIALOGUE!*

MAD

FULL BLAZING COLOR

FULL BLAZING COLOR!

STAR WARS SPECTACULAR

THE ORIGINAL TRILOGY! THE *STAR* WARS MUSICAL! AND MUCH MORE!

(Did we mention that Every Page is in Full Blazing Color?)

SUMMER 1999 $2.99 CHEAP!

UNITED STATES

MAD Star Wars Spectacular, Summer 1999
Cover, *Star Wars* Characters' Bodies Spelling Out "*Star Wars*"
(Artist: Mort Drucker)

HERE WE GO WITH ANOTHER RIDICULOUS
MAD FOLD-IN

These days if something is hugely popular, chances are a sequel will be made with the hope that the second will be just as profitable as the first. There is, however, one sequel coming this summer that will try and probably fail to top itself. To find out what this sequel is, fold page in as shown...

FOLD PAGE OVER LIKE THIS!

A ◄ FOLD PAGE OVER LEFT   B FOLD BACK SO "A" MEETS "B"

STAR PERFORMERS ALWAYS LIKE TO REPEAT THE HOT ROLES THEY'VE PLAYED SO FANS WILL COME RUSHING IN TO SEE THEM ONCE AGAIN. BUT IN REALITY THIS VERY SELDOM EVER TAKES PLACE

A   ARTIST AND WRITER: AL JAFFEE   B

NO NEED TO RUIN YOUR BOOK BY FOLDING THIS PAGE! JUST TURN TO THE NEXT PAGE TO SEE THE ANSWER!

MAD #381, May 1999
Fold-in, "What Epic Struggle Will Resume This Summer but Fail to Live Up to Its Predecessor?"

MCGWIRE AND SOSA SUCCUMB TO THE DARK SIDE

Since this Fold-in was published, Mark McGwire and Sammy Sosa have been brought low by steroid and bat-corking scandals. However, if Darth Vader redeemed himself by throwing the Emperor into the Death Star's reactor core, maybe McGwire and Sosa can rehabilitate themselves by doing the same to Pete Rose.

WHAT EPIC STRUGGLE WILL RESUME THIS SUMMER BUT FAIL TO LIVE UP TO ITS PREDECESSOR?

FOLD PAGE OVER LIKE THIS!

A ◄►B FOLD BACK SO "A" MEETS "B"

MAC 70
SOSA 66

THE HOME RUN RACE
A ◄►B

MAD #381, May 1999
Fold-in FOLDED!

COUNTDOWN TO...
THE PHANTOM MENACE

...A ridiculous recap of the inane, insipid and insignificant incidents leading up to the most highly anticipated movie of all time!*

*excluding Weekend At Bernie's II

MARCH 11

Lucasfilm representatives say the security surrounding *The Phantom Menace* is the tightest ever for a motion picture. They assure the press that no unauthorized persons will see the film until it opens May 19th.

MARCH 16

Pirated VHS copies of *The Phantom Menace* go on sale in Hong Kong for $10.

ARTIST: AMANDA CONNER
WRITER: CHARLIE KADAU

MARCH 23

Entertainment Weekly presents a special issue: *The 100 Greatest Storm Troopers From The Original Star Wars Trilogy*. Topping the list — the one that shoots at Han Solo in *The Empire Strikes Back*, followed by the one Luke shoots in *Star Wars* and then the one Leia pushes over a ledge in *Return of the Jedi*, plus 97 more!

MARCH 31

George Lucas signs one of the most lucrative (and strangest) fast-food cross-promotion deals ever. To get a *Phantom Menace* action toy, you will have to buy a hamburger at McDonald's, bring it to a Burger King for the ketchup and pickles, swing by a Wendy's for the French fries, and finally, drop in at an Arby's for a super-sized cup of Clamato. Despite this, the action toys sell out in less than a week.

"PIRATED VHS COPIES OF THE PHANTOM MENACE"

When producer Rick McCallum went on a world tour of many of the international premieres of *The Phantom Menace* during the summer of 1999, he'd often be mobbed by fans asking him to sign bootleg copies, usually before the film had even been released in that country. In one Eastern European nation, McCallum claims to have discovered the movie already playing in his hotel. This suggests that if you want to see any future *Star Wars* projects weeks before their official openings, try checking into an Eastern European hotel—they're probably already showing them!

MAD #383, July 1999
"Countdown to . . . *The Phantom Menace*"

TRUE STORIES FROM THE FAN LINEUP

Here's another example of how *MAD* can't top a world gone mad: A couple of fans in Seattle lined up for Episode III in January 2005. The movie was coming out in May. Even worse, they lined up in front of the wrong theater.

"C3P OH NO!"

While there are no confirmed reports of Obi-Wan Kenobi having a "thing" for C-3PO, actor Jake Lloyd (young Anakin Skywalker) remembers being "shocked" by seeing Ewan McGregor lick Yoda's ear on the set.

MAY 19

THEATER

PHANTOM MENACE

FOOTLOOSE II

The film has received so much pre-release hype that everybody figures they'll be smart, skip the opening weekend mobs and go in a week or two. *Star Wars: The Phantom Menace* has an opening weekend gross of only $6.2 million, one of the weakest in history, trailing *The Postman* and even *Eight Heads in a Duffel Bag*.

MAY 14

Jay Leno makes the inevitable joke that Samuel L. Jackson's big scene in the movie is when he asks Yoda if he knows what a Quarter Pounder is called on Tatooine.

MAY 13

Dennis Miller makes the inevitable joke that Samuel L. Jackson's big scene in the movie is when he asks Yoda if he knows what a Quarter Pounder is called on Tatooine.

MAY

MAY 11

entertainment WEEKLY

TOP 100 STORM TROOPERS

PRINCESS LEIA'S FAMOUS DOS

ANAKIN SKYWALKER'S $2.8 MILLION PLAYROOM

OBI-WAN & C3PO?

LUCAS & HIS LHASAS INSPIRATION FOR EWOKS?

THE MANY GIRLFRIENDS OF R2-D2

Entertainment Weekly presents a special issue: *The 100 Greatest Articles We've run on The Phantom Menace* this year.

APRIL 30

The Ain't It Cool News Website takes a blow to its credibility when its highly-promoted secret stills of the creepy new aliens from the movie turn out to be nothing more than nude pictures of Dr. Laura Schlessinger.

MAY 3

While appearing on *Live With Regis and Kathie Lee*, actor Ewan McGregor takes part in a light saber demonstration that goes horribly wrong. The next day's show is the first with its new name, *Live With Regis*.

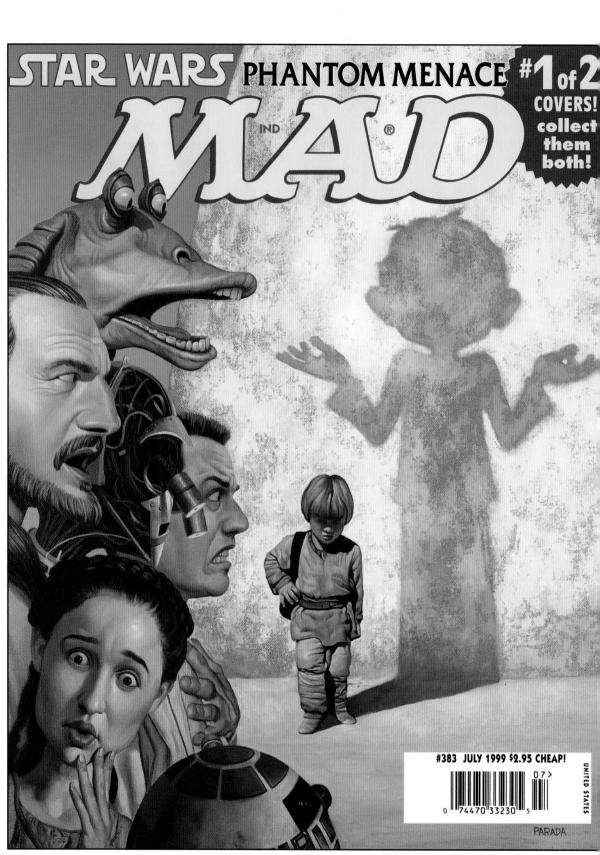

MAD #383, July 1999
Collector Covers Parodying the Episode I Poster
(Artist: Roberto Parada)

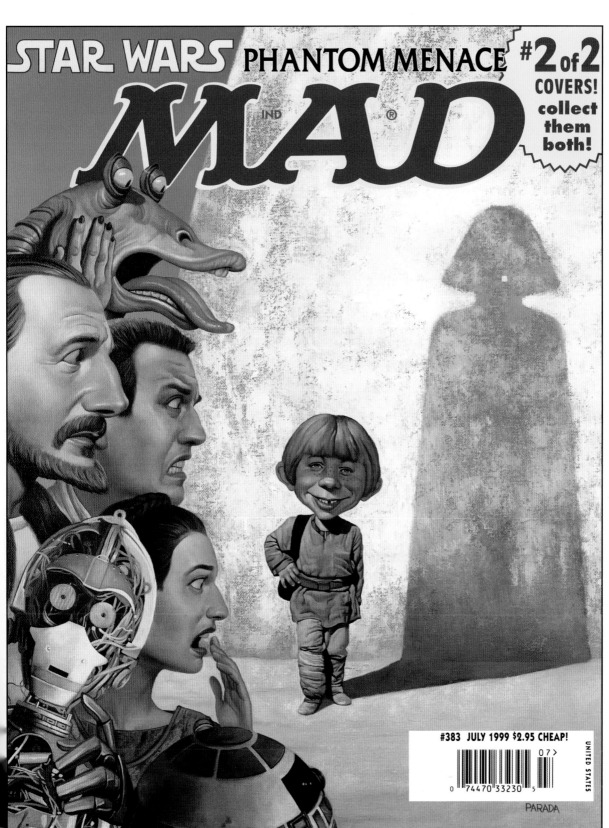

#383 JULY 1999 $2.95 CHEAP!

0 74470 33230 5

07>

UNITED STATES

PARADA

SHADOW PLAY

According to Jim Ward, president of LucasArts and senior vice president of Lucasfilm, when he was developing the Episode I poster campaign, he felt that the "shadow of Vader" concept that artist Ellen Moon Lee created did the best job of concisely capturing what the "prequel" was in terms of its place in the overall *Star Wars* saga. This poster ended up being the first image of the prequels seen by the public. It caused a media frenzy and was soon all over the Internet as well as newspapers, magazines, and television. Seeing *MAD* choose this particular image out of the multitude of possible scenes to parody confirmed to Ward and Lee the effectiveness of this poster.

The "shadow of Vader" poster.

It seems that good old George Lucas didn't make enough billions off the hordes of *Star Wars* fans out there. Nope, even with all the movies, toys, costumes and videos, some flunky in George's marketing department told him that there was a few bucks more to be drained out of his most loyal fans. So before you could say Obi Wan Kenobi, out came a special edition of the game *Trivial Pursuit* chock full of mind-numbing questions about Luke, Darth and the boys. Think you know everything about *Star Wars* just because you've seen the trilogy "about a zillion times?" Don't bet on it, Yoda Breath! Prepare to feel the farce in...

MAD's STAR

YO • Where did the Death Star's thermal exhaust port lead directly to?

UAR • According to Obi Wan, what can have a "strong influence on the weak minded?"

EAB • According to the trailer for *Episode 1 – The Phantom Menace*, "every saga has what"?

IG • Why were Luke and Leia hidden at birth, according to Obi Wan?

MOR • Who told Luke "you can't hide forever"?

ON • Luke was urged to feel what?

MAD's STAR WARS Trivial Pursuit

YO Bayonne, New Jersey

UAR Scientology

EAB Several licensable characters

IG To beat the hospital charges

MOR Salman Rushdie

ON Obi Wan's goiter

TOO MUCH INFORMATION DEPARTMENT

Anthony Daniels has the card from the real *Star Wars* Trivial Pursuit that asks who played C-3PO framed in his bathroom. Unfortunately, he doesn't have the German *Star Wars* toilet paper. (Some people at Lucas Licensing used to joke that the tagline for that particular product was going to be "wipe out the dark side.")

German *Star Wars* toilet paper.
Photo by Anne Neumann.
© Lucasfilm Ltd. & TM. All rights reserved.

YO • Who was described as "being more machine than man"?

UAR • What did Han yell after he blasted the Death Star?

EAB • What event caused "a great disturbance in the Force" according to Obi Wan?

IG • What did Luke not know the power of, according to Darth Vader?

MOR • According to Yoda, what does a Jedi never use the Force for?

ON • Who played Chewbacca in all three movies?

MAD's STAR WARS Trivial Pursuit

YO Al Gore

UAR "I'm goin' to DisneyWorld!"

EAB Jabba's indigestion

IG The Toy Licensees

MOR To win at the craps tables in Vegas

ON Barbra Streisand

ARTIST: HERMANN MEJIA   WRITER: J. PRETE

MAD #383, July 1999
"*MAD's Star Wars* Trivial Pursuit"

WARS *Trivial Pursuit*

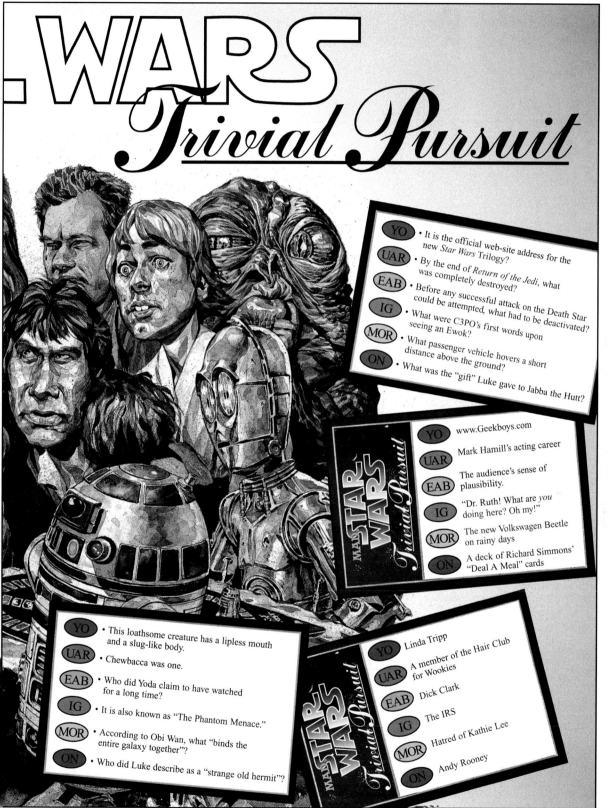

YO • It is the official web-site address for the new *Star Wars* Trilogy?

UAR • By the end of *Return of the Jedi*, what was completely destroyed?

EAB • Before any successful attack on the Death Star could be attempted, what had to be deactivated?

IG • What were C3PO's first words upon seeing an Ewok?

MOR • What passenger vehicle hovers a short distance above the ground?

ON • What was the "gift" Luke gave to Jabba the Hutt?

MAD STAR WARS Trivial Pursuit

YO www.Geekboys.com

UAR Mark Hamill's acting career

EAB The audience's sense of plausibility.

IG "Dr. Ruth! What are *you* doing here? Oh my!"

MOR The new Volkswagen Beetle on rainy days

ON A deck of Richard Simmons' "Deal A Meal" cards

YO • This loathsome creature has a lipless mouth and a slug-like body.

UAR • Chewbacca was one.

EAB • Who did Yoda claim to have watched for a long time?

IG • It is also known as "The Phantom Menace."

MOR • According to Obi Wan, what "binds the entire galaxy together"?

ON • Who did Luke describe as a "strange old hermit"?

MAD STAR WARS Trivial Pursuit

YO Linda Tripp

UAR A member of the Hair Club for Wookies

EAB Dick Clark

IG The IRS

MOR Hatred of Kathie Lee

ON Andy Rooney

BACKSEAT ARTISTS

Artist Hermann Mejia was a huge fan of Mort Drucker's classic *Star Wars* parodies, and he studied them intently as a kid growing up in Venezuela. When he got this assignment from *MAD*, it was his first chance to spoof *Star Wars*, and he was extremely excited— so much so that he told all his friends. This proved to be a bit of a mistake, as they spent the entire time he was working on this piece looking over his shoulder telling him how to depict the characters.

MAD's
CELEBRITY CAUSE-OF-DEATH
BETTING ODDS

Our team of crack oddsmakers gives you the latest Vegas line
on how one of today's biggest stars will go to the Dark Side!

THIS MONTH'S BANTHA FODDER TO BE:

ARTIST: HERMANN MEJIA
WRITER: MIKE SNIDER

GEORGE LUCAS

CAUSE OF DEATH	ODDS
Smothered in hugs and kisses at toy manufacturers' convention	3:1
Executed by mob of nit-picking Star Wars nerds over mistakes, plot holes and logic inconsistencies in first trilogy	5:1
Bludgeoned to death by embittered Mark Hamill for not giving him even a bit part in the new trilogy	20:1
Fatal skin rash from wearing the same plaid lumberjack shirt since 1975	25:1
Excessive worrying about availability of financing for next film project	200,879:1

ACTION FIGURES

As a child, artist Hermann Mejia begged his father to buy him *Star Wars* action figures, Yoda in particular. However, his father kept buying him stormtroopers because they were made with more plastic, but sold for the same price as Yoda, and thus seemed like a better deal to the elder Mejia. As a result, Hermann had legions of stormtroopers and no other characters. Thus, when doing this illustration, Hermann was happy to throw in some non-stormtrooper characters (seen at the bottom of the page).

A vintage Kenner stormtrooper.
Photo by Anne Neumann.

MAD #383, July 1999
"*MAD*'s Celebrity Cause-of-Death Betting Odds: George Lucas"

HERE WE GO WITH ANOTHER RIDICULOUS
MAD FOLD-IN

There are few events that manage to excite people all over the world. Even major holidays like Christmas or Passover do not apply to all cultures. But there is one occurrence that is universally celebrated. To find out what this event is, fold page in as shown.

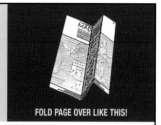

FOLD PAGE OVER LIKE THIS!

A ◄ FOLD PAGE OVER LEFT   **B** FOLD BACK SO THAT "A" MEETS "B"

THE LONG AWAITED DAY FINALLY ARRIVES AND VAST
DELEGATIONS OF KIDS REJOICE. THEIR WAY OF
CELEBRATING IS LEGENDARY. ON EVERYONE'S
SCHEDULE THIS IS ONE EVENT THAT'S VERY COOL

A   ARTIST AND WRITER: AL JAFFEE   **B**

*NO NEED TO RUIN
YOUR BOOK BY
FOLDING THIS PAGE!
JUST TURN TO THE
NEXT PAGE TO SEE
THE ANSWER!*

MAD #383, July 1999
Fold-in, "What Eagerly Anticipated Event Is Finally Upon Us?"

STAR WARS RELEASE AS HOLIDAY

The fact that MAD could base a Fold-in around the idea that the release of a Star Wars movie is a holiday on par with Christmas or the last day of school is a testament, of course, to how "sacred" Star Wars became to the culture at large.

MAD #383, July 1999
Fold-in FOLDED!

Celine Dion's voice mail number: Leave message asking her if she wants role of Mrs. Binks in Episode 2.

10 AM: Meet with California State Legislature, propose bill to have "Gungan" taught in public schools.

Have Harrison Ford fix my porch.

Meet with Italian Anti-Defamation League over my plans to introduce space teamster character named "Wop-Wop."

Synchronize and back up my Palm V Organizer with my PC with just one touch — hey, I wonder how many millions I could make if I slapped a sticker of Queen Amidala on this thing and sold it as a Star Wars toy?

Address Book
Date Book
Memo Pad
To Do List
HotSync

3Con
Moronically connected.

George Lucas
Filmmaker; Visionary; Prophet

Palm™

Memo 1 of 5

• Celine Dion as Mrs. Jar Jar Binks in Episode II?!
• How to thank John "Battlefield Earth" Travolta for taking heat off Phantom Menace as worst sci-fi flick of all time?? Flowers? Candy?
• Episode 1: Computer-generated creatures
• Episode 2: Sock puppets! (Talk to boys at ILM)

(Done) (Details)

Forcefully Palm

www.palmed-off.con

Palm Conartists, Inc., developer of the world's leading ill-conceived handheld toy.
©2000 Forcefully Palm and the Palm logo are trademarks of Palmed-Off, Inc., which means nothing to you who will no doubt end up mistaking it for the freakin' channel-changer anyway!

SHILLING FOR THE FORCE

"George" here is portrayed by Sam Viviano, *MAD*'s art director. He doesn't have a sixty-five-hundred-acre ranch in Marin County, but he has a nice little co-op on the Upper West Side and brings in Girl Scout cookies for the staff to munch on. Lucas, meanwhile, has actually done commercials, but only in Japan, and part of his deal is that they never be shown in the States. In fact, Lucas is perhaps more of a celebrity over there than he is here. According to president of Lucas Licensing, Howard Roffman, parts of Sofia Coppola's *Lost in Translation* were influenced by her experience on the *Phantom Menace* press tour in Japan (Coppola played Saché, one of Amidala's handmaidens). Like Bill Murray's character, Bob Harris, Lucas endured the bizarre Japanese talk-show circuit, which actually made him wear a rice-paddy straw hat. If anyone in Japan is reading this, we expect you to put that up on YouTube posthaste!

MAD art director Sam Viviano.

MAD #400, December 2000
"Forcefully Palm"

MAULFRED E. NEUMAN

Iain McCaig, the artist who designed Darth Maul, exclaimed that seeing his creation on the cover of *MAD* was better than winning an Oscar. Below, you can see the cover go through its various phases of development—from an initial sketch by editor Nick Meglin, to a digital comp by art director Sam Viviano, to painter Mark Stutzman's preliminary pencils. You can also see all the international versions of this cover on the opposite page.

The evolution of the Alfred-as-Darth-Maul cover.

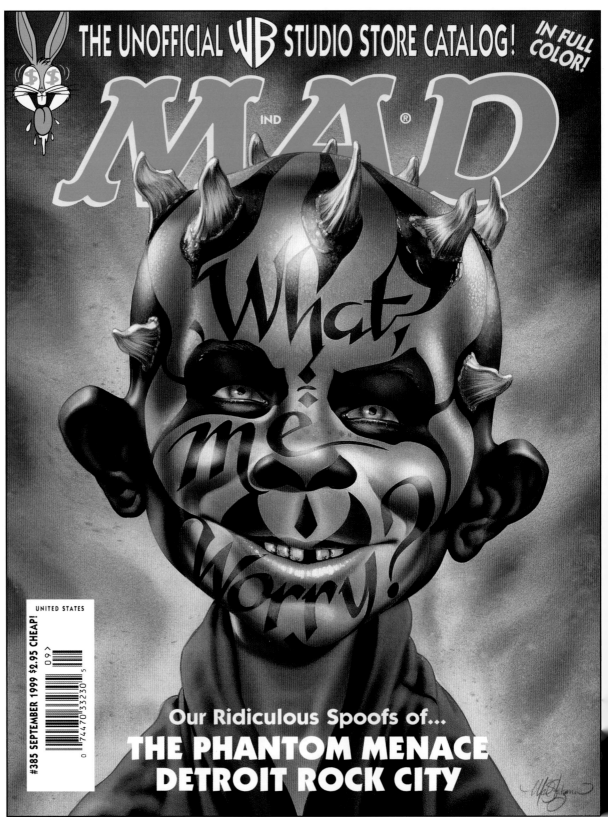

MAD #385, September 1999
Cover, Alfred as Darth Maul
(Artist: Mark Stutzman)

GERMANY SURRENDERS

Note the modifications the Brazilian and Swedish editions of *MAD* made to the tattoo pattern in order to get their respective catchphrases to fit on Alfred's face. The German *MAD*, however, seems to have figured that it wasn't worth the effort.

Australia

Brazil

Finland

Germany

India

Sweden

Turmoil has engulfed the movie industry as legions desperately await the next Star Bores epic. Hoping to resolve the matter, greedy director George Lucas begins filming while dispatching his lawyers to sign merchandising deals throughout the galaxy. As the geeks endlessly debate who's cooler, Darth Maul or Boba Fett, moviegoers everywhere waste hours waiting on line, only to discover that after all the hype, this story-free, poorly-acted flick's nothing more than…

I'm **QuiteGone Jim**, Jet-Eye Master! I am **closely attuned** to the **living Force**, but I follow a **different path** than most Jet-Eyes! I made sure I got **killed off** in the **FIRST** of these three lame flicks!

I'm the **young Oldie Von Moldie**! I've **nearly completed** all my **training** as a Jet-Eye apprentice! As a matter of fact, I'm so **close** to **graduating**, I've already had my **picture taken** for the **yearbook**! I was voted "**Most Likely to Succeed in Sequels**"! As part of my **Jet-Eye** training, I built this **light saber** with my **own hands**! It can **cut** through anything… except the **overblown special effects** to this **overdone** story!

I'm **Death Hideous** from the **Dark Side**! I inspire an **unsettling sense** of **dread**, like those "You have **performed** an **illegal action**" blurbs that suddenly **spring up** on our **super-sophisticated computer screens** when you haven't done a thing! My **lifelong dream** is to put an **end** to all **peace-loving Jet-Eye Knights**! I spread **evil** via **holographic transmissions** from my **headquarters** on **Croissant** — and to **really** annoy folks, I send 'em **COLLECT!**

I'm **Mannequin Skystalker**, apprentice to **Jet-Eye Master QuiteGone Jim!** Even at my **young age**, I can feel the **Force** within me! Either that, or it's **puberty** kicking in a little **early!** I'm also in **training** to be a **loyal** and **obedient Jet-Eye!** Already I learned how to **roll over, beg**, and **fetch** a light saber! To be a Jet-Eye, I had to **abandon my mother** so that in the **future**, I can become the **father** of **Lube Skystalker** and **Princess Laidup!** Pretty **confusing**, considering that **everybody** knows how this **cash-milking** saga ends!

I'm **Shamu**, Mannequin Skystalker's **mother!** I know this **sounds strange**, but Mannequin **doesn't have a father!** I guess you could call it an **immaculate MIS-conception!** Oh, okay, so I **did** have a **husband**, but he made me **promise** I'd **never tell anyone** who **fathered** such a rotten little actor!

I'm **Queen AmaDilly**, leader of the **No BooBoo Nation!** When I was **younger**, I wanted to be either a **fashion model** or the **ruler** of a **small nation!** This is the **perfect combination** — I rule a **small, starving** nation AND I'm **emaciated** and wear lots of **weird clothes!** My **vow** is to keep **NoBooBoo** a **peace-loving** place, no matter how many **battles** and **blood baths** it takes to do it!

ARTIST: MORT DRUCKER   WRITER: DICK DEBARTOLO

HOISTING THE HEADDRESS

According to costume designer Trisha Bigger, this headdress had to be hooked up to a pulley made of fishing wire that was looped up through the set's light rigging to help Natalie Portman support the weight. Insert your own Donald Trump gag here.

The heavy headdress.

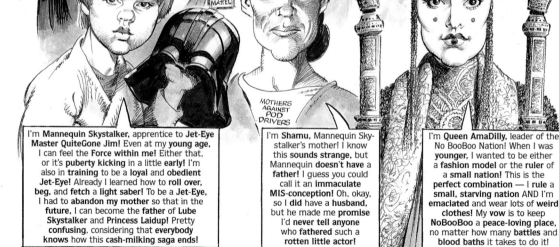

MAD #385, September 1999
"Star Bores: Epic Load I The Fandumb Megamess"

STAR BORES
EPIC LOAD I
THE FANDUMB MEGAMESS

I'm **Creepio**, a droid on the planet of **Tattoo!** Believe it or not, I was made from a **huge mess** of **wires** by **nine-year-old Mannequin Skystalker!** In effect, he was my **father!** My **mother** was a **plate of spaghetti!**

I'm **Death Mall**, and I wield a **double-bladed light saber!** It's not quite as good as that **triple-bladed Gillette Mach 3**, but I can give my opponents a **damn close shave** anyway! I revel in the **evil** of the **Dark Side!** My scary **tattooed face, glowing evil eyes** and **horned skull** mean only one thing: **KISS** just might be able to **stage a comeback** after all! Don't **believe me?** See **page 43!**

I'm **Har Har Blinks**, a **Gungun! Gunguns** are **extremely intelligent** beings, which is kinda **hard to believe** since we all **tawlk** wike **liddle baybees** wid **iwrating voices**, like **Baabaa Walters** on **speed!** Truswt **mee**, a **liddle Gungun** goes a **roooong waay!!**

I am **Lace Windows**, the only **black senior member** of the **Jet-Eye Council!** Actually, that **isn't bad**, when you consider that the **other members** are mostly **green, yellow** and **magenta!** As a **senior member** I no longer wield my **blue-bladed light saber** and I **don't get to say** a **heck of a lot!** But I do **enjoy a 10% senior citizen's discount** at the **Jet-Eye commissary** and **gift shop!**

MAY THIS HORSE BE WITH YOU!

FORCE BE WITH YOU MAY THE

PULP SCIENCE FICTION

I'm **Bar Stool!** I was a **sort of glorified garbage can** in *Star Bores IV, V, and VI!* But now it's **years earlier**, so I'm an **earlier version!** I'm **just like the later model**, only **without** the **driver's side airbag** and **automatic pencil sharpener!**

Yodel I am, a **senior member** of the **Jet-Eye council!** Famous I am for over **800 years** of dispensing wisdom! I was the one who **proclaimed:** "The **Dark Side** is hard to see in a **dim light**"! And "Why do they call it a **light saber** when it **weighs ten pounds?**" Find these **wise**, you do not? Well, **800 years** old I am! Gems they all **cannot** be!

I'm **Pikachu!** Although I'm **not** in this **movie**, I'm here to **learn** from a **master!** No, not a **Jet-Eye master!** I'm talking about **George Lucas** — a **merchandising master!**

R2-D2'S "DRIVER'S SIDE AIRBAG"

In the 1980s *Star Wars* animated series *Droids*, R2-D2 actually does have an air bag. He also break-dances. No joke. Lucasfilm Internet content manager Pablo Hidalgo invites you to check out an inventory of R2-D2's abilities at www.starwars.com/kids/explore/eu/f20041116/index.html

R2-D2 deploying his air bag.

R2-D2 break-dancing.

"WHY NOT JUST USE MY MIND POWER TO SEND A MASSIVE HEART ATTACK TO DEATH MALL!"

Once again, *MAD* points out a logic flaw. After all, if Darth Vader can choke people right and left without going near them, why waste time with all the lightsaber fights? On the other hand, it's probably a lot easier for toy stores to sell lightsabers than heart attacks.

A MAD LOOK AT STAR WARS EPISODE I THE PHANTOM MENACE

THE HYPE

ARTIST AND WRITER: SERGIO ARAGONES

MAD #385, September 1999
"A MAD Look at Star Wars: Episode I The Phantom Menace: The Hype"

ANOTHER TRUE STORY FROM THE FAN LINEUP

Director of content management and fan relations Steve Sansweet tells another story of fans lining up early. Apparently about six weeks before Episode III opened, a group of fans started lining up outside the famed Grauman's Chinese Theatre in LA. Unfortunately, the theater had been acquired by Paramount and wasn't going to show Star Wars, a Twentieth Century Fox movie. Sansweet relayed this to the fans. The fans, however, refused to believe him. After all, they argued, every other Star Wars movie had played there, and they still had hope. Sansweet had a bit of a situation on his hands—there were all these Star Wars fans crowding the theater for a movie that would never open there, and they wouldn't leave. Finally he worked something out. The day of the midnight premiere of the film, a large parade was orchestrated in which the legions of fans who had lined up in front of Grauman's Chinese Theatre marched the mile to ArcLight Cinemas. This "Million Nerd March" was probably the most exercise they'd had in the last ten years.

THE KAADU/ KADAU CONFUSION

In the third strip from the top, we see a child asking for a toy of a Gungan warrior riding a kaadu. For a time, *MAD* senior editor Charlie Kadau entertained the idea that perhaps I had a role in naming the creature after him. I, however, had done no such thing, as I had been busy trying to figure out (unsuccessfully) how to get Lucas to name things after *me*!

The beast of burden above is a kaadu, not to be confused with *MAD* senior editor Charlie Kadau (below), who looks more like an Ewok anyway.

Photo by Irving Schild.

STAR WARS HOOKY

Here we see Aragonés depicting a man skipping out on work to see Episode I. This was actually a pretty common occurrence. According to a CNN article written around the time of Episode I's release, an employment firm had estimated that about 2.2 million people were going to skip work to see the film the day it came out. In order to avoid this, one company was reported to have bought tickets to the midnight showing for its employees in exchange for them showing up to work the next day. Another firm simply threw up its hands and gave employees the day off. Meanwhile, according to the BBC, for Episode III, a U.S. consulting firm estimated that that film's release could cost $627 million in lost productivity. It could have been even worse, but Aragonés was actually *going to work* by seeing the film, thus helping the U.S. economy avert disaster.

SERGE-IN GENERAL DEPT.

A MAD LOOK AT THE

ARTIST AND WRITER: SERGIO ARAGONES

SERGIO ARAGONÉS'S PROCESS

In order to do gags about a movie, Sergio Aragonés must go see the film three or four times. The first time, he sees it without taking notes so he can pay attention to everything that is happening. The second time, he takes notes on the plot, and the third and fourth times, he works on the gags. Or so he says. It's also possible he just likes seeing movies again and again on *MAD*'s dime.

MAD #385, September 1999
"A MAD Look at The Phantom Menace"

PHANTOM MENACE

SEBULBA'S PODRACER

According to ILM visual effects supervisor John Knoll, there are certain shots in the Podrace where there is no one piloting Sebulba's racer because the effects team forgot to put him in there. Apparently digital actors don't fight for more screen time.

STAR WARS TOYS

Star Wars toys actually do make appearances in the films. According to Don Bies, veteran ILM model shop member and R2-D2 operator, little painted figures from Galoob's *Star Wars* MicroMachines sets were used in some of *The Phantom Menace*'s Podrace crowd shots. Furthermore, Bies reports, in *The Empire Strikes Back*, when Luke vaults out of the carbon freezing chamber, an action figure was actually used. Finally, according to model maker Lorne Peterson, in some of the Episode II arena battle scenes, because the action figures had been manufactured before the visual effects were finished, ILM used them to shoot the scenes that the figures were supposedly based on. For its next project, Lucasfilm is considering doing a casting call at Toys "R" Us.

BEHEADING BINKS

Another example of *Star Wars* showing up in *MAD*'s "20 Dumbest People, Events & Things" of the year. However, unlike "Starr Wars" (page 65) where the film is simply a vehicle used to mock the Lewinsky affair, here *Star Wars*—and Jar Jar Binks in particular—is itself the target.

The backlash against Jar Jar was so extreme that George Lucas decided to have a little fun with it, putting EPISODE II *JAR JAR'S BIG ADVENTURE* on the cover sheet of his handwritten script and the typed versions that were distributed. Poor Jar Jar couldn't catch a break.

While Ahmed Best, the actor who played Jar Jar on the set and whose movements were motion-captured for the Jar Jar CG model, might have something of a point when he says that people may have been projecting their own pre-conceived notions onto the character, *MAD* thought decapitating the Gungan was funnier than having a nuanced debate.

While we are on the subject of the much-maligned Mr. Binks, I have to elaborate on the confession I made in the introduction regarding my tenure as a proto-Jar Jar. Basically, during pre-production on Episode I, whenever someone awkward, lanky, and clumsy was needed for some rough, temporary Jar Jar Binks footage, I was pressed into service. (Note to the anti-Jar Jar crowd: His dialogue hadn't been worked on yet, so don't start sending me hate mail!)

Here I am as a proto-Jar Jar Binks.
From video footage by Ben Burtt.

20 JAR-JAR BINKS **INTERGALACTIC STEPIN FETCHIT**

Leave it to George "Don't-Forget-He-Also-Made-*Howard-the-Duck*" Lucas to actually come up with a character more irritating than the Ewoks! Even more impressive, Jar-Jar Binks pulled off the improbable feat of offending three social groups who for many years have endured society's intolerance: blacks, gays and *Star Wars* geeks. How wude! We can only hope that by 2002, George will let us know The Force is again with him by releasing

A MOVIE POSTER WE'D ALL LIKE TO SEE

STAR WARS
EPISODE II
A GALAXY REJOICES

MAD #389, June 2000
"Jar-Jar Binks: Intergalactic Stepin Fetchit"

As we all eagerly await the release of Star Wars Episode II: Attack of the Clones, we also all eagerly await word on what the heck the darn movie's about. Director George Lucas has been extremely secretive about the plot, but we've managed to find out that it apparently revolves around clones who attack someone (and may even be attacked themselves)! Unfortunately, aside from this scoop, we've come up empty, and offer you instead…

THE 21 HOTTEST
INTERNET RUMORS
REGARDING
STAR WARS
EPISODE II:
ATTACK OF THE CLONES

ARTIST: HERMANN MEJIA   WRITER: ARIE KAPLAN

STILL ANOTHER R2-D2 TRASH CAN GAG
Told you you'd see this gag yet again!

MAD #418, June 2002
"The 21 Hottest Internet Rumors Regarding *Star Wars* Episode II: *Attack of the Clones*"

THE 21 HOTTEST INTERNET RUMORS REGARDING STAR WARS EPISODE II: ATTACK OF THE CLONES

2 The entire movie is dubbed into an obscure Naboo dialect, with Huttese subtitles at the bottom of the screen, and a window in the top right corner in which an interpreter provides Gungan sign language.

Dopo mee gusha, peedunkey?

1 A new space-pimp character, "Shutt Yo-Mowff," was deemed inappropriate and cut from the film; character is scheduled to have his own series on UPN.

3 Foreshadowing his move to the Dark Side, Anakin reacts violently when he's told that "got your nose" is not a Jedi mind trick.

4 In a controversial move by the Republic, former space sitcom stars ALF and Mork from Ork are granted seats on the Jedi Council.

5 We're finally treated to a translation of the Wookiee language, and we learn that whenever a Wookiee roars, it means, "Kiss my hairy ass!"

6 In a cost-saving move, Jabba The Hutt's court is replaced by a gaggle of melting Nazis who just opened the Ark of the Covenant.

7 Anakin first expresses his interest in Amidala when he uses The Force to undo her bra.

8 Proving beyond a shadow of a doubt that the film's editor was asleep at the wheel, there's a scene in which Anakin is present at his own birth.

9 Anakin's sexual naiveté contributes to his impregnating Amidala; while having sex with her, he puts a condom on his light saber.

CONDOMS

Over the years Lucasfilm has received numerous pitches for condoms, says Lucas Licensing president Howard Roffman. Specifically, black Darth Vader condoms. One can only imagine the "Feel the Force" ad campaign.

10 Obi-Wan incites a bloody interplanetary war when, at a cocktail party for the Prime Minister of Rigel 4, he eats a creamy, delicious pudding, which turn out to *be* the Prime Minister of Rigel 4.

THE 21 HOTTEST INTERNET RUMORS REGARDING STAR WARS

EPISODE II: ATTACK OF THE CLONES

11 The scene with Geraldo reporting from war-torn Tatooine is left on cutting room floor, just like 'N Sync.

12 After having already seen the forest planet, the ice planet, the swamp planet, the cloud planet, the city planet and the water planet, we're finally treated to the papier-mâché planet, which goes up in flames when Yoda unexpectedly lights a cigar.

13 In the film's scariest moment, R2D2 is captured by a giant ogre and used as a stick of roll-on deodorant.

R2-D2 DEODORANT
Believe it or not, according to Steve Sansweet, there has never been an R2-D2 roll-on deodorant. Of course, with the new *Star Wars* TV shows coming out, there's still a chance.

14 In some sort of intergalactic *Crying Game* homage, Queen Amidala takes off her Kabuki makeup...and she's a dude!

15 Lucas got the idea for clones after seeing an E! special on the Baldwin Brothers.

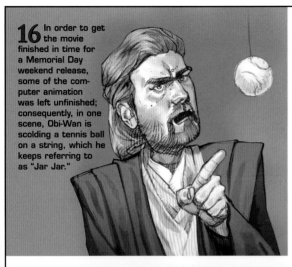

16 In order to get the movie finished in time for a Memorial Day weekend release, some of the computer animation was left unfinished; consequently, in one scene, Obi-Wan is scolding a tennis ball on a string, which he keeps referring to as "Jar Jar."

17 Lucas fired his set decorator mid-production when it was discovered that all of his matte paintings of alien landscapes were actually plagiarized Yes album covers from the early 1970s.

18 While intergalactic gangster Jabba the Hutt marries off his daughter, a nervous gelatinous cube sits outside the palace rehearsing the following speech: "It is my honor to be invited to your daughter's wedding, Donn Hutt. May the first child be a morbidly-obese child."

19 In hopes of attracting an even larger teen audience, Lucas added a scene in which Obi-Wan walks in on Anakin trying to hump a Carpathian cream pie.

20 Jimmy Smits plays Princess Leia's adoptive father and Dennis Franz makes a cameo as his partner, Eig, a trash-talking, unorthodox space-cop from the planet Zimbo.

21 In a blatant example of product placement we are introduced to a trio of new characters: X-BOX, TiVO and SUV.

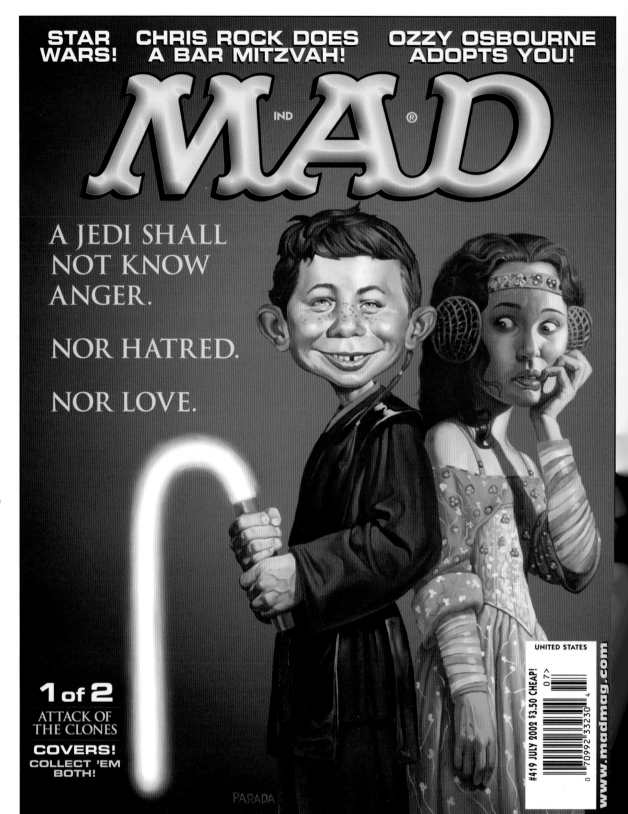

**MEL BROOKS
BEAT US TO IT**
After *MAD* did this suggestive lightsaber gag, it was pointed out that Mel Brooks did a variation on it first in *Spaceballs*. Oops!

MAD #419, July 2002
Collector Cover Parodying *Attack of the Clones*
(Artist: Roberto Parada)

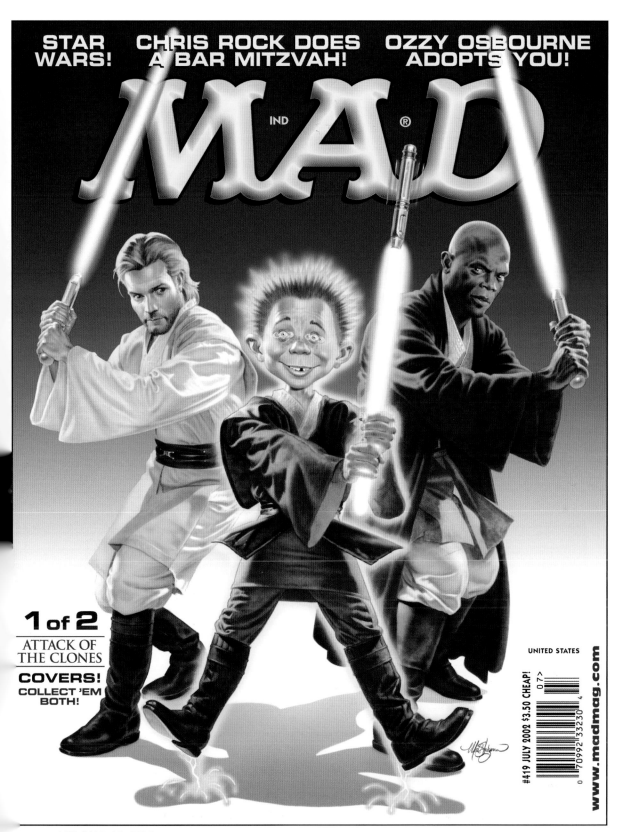

STAR WARS! CHRIS ROCK DOES A BAR MITZVAH! OZZY OSBOURNE ADOPTS YOU!

MAD

IND

®

1 of 2
ATTACK OF
THE CLONES

COVERS!
COLLECT 'EM
BOTH!

UNITED STATES

#419 JULY 2002 $3.50 CHEAP!

07>

www.madmag.com

0 70992 33230 4

MAD #419, July 2002
Collector Cover Parodying *Attack of the Clones*
(Artist: Mark Stutzman)

JOKE AND DAGGER DEPT.

MOVIE-INSPIRED SPIES

Spy Vs. Spy adventures are rarely inspired by movies. However, you can find a *Spider-Man* episode in *MAD* #444, August 2004, and a *Pirates of the Caribbean* one in *MAD* #479, July 2007.

ARTIST AND WRITER: PETER KUPER

MAD #419, July 2002
"Spy Vs. Spy: *Star Wars: Attack of the Clones*"

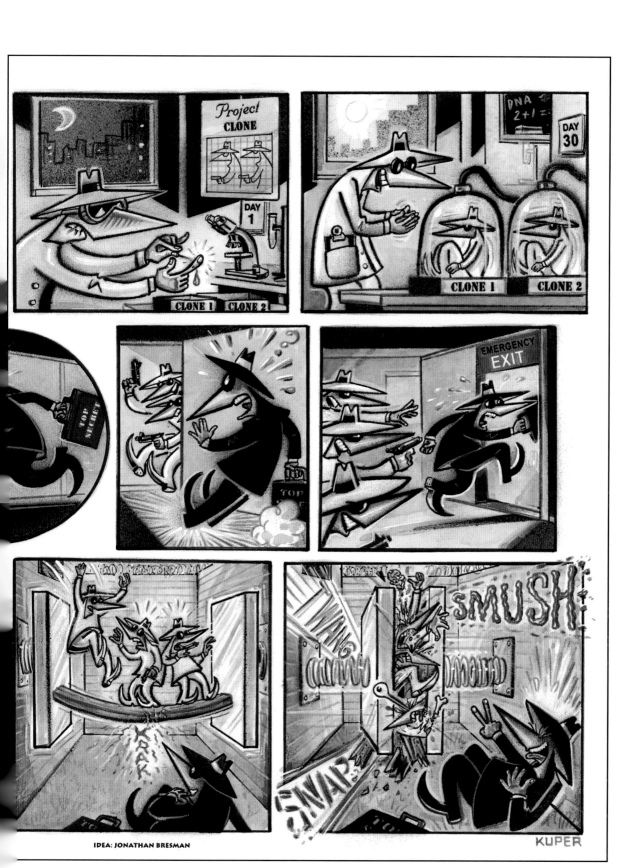

IDEA: JONATHAN BRESMAN

KUPER

Call us crazy, but it seems that the characters in *Star Wars Episode II: Attack of the Clones* are beginning to remind us of television's most popular family — no, not the Osbournes, Ewok head, the Bradys! There's the handsome Greg Brady type who's always getting into trouble (Anakin), the pretty Marcia Brady type who's always changing her outfits (Padmé), the well-meaning but kind of dull dad Mike Brady type (Obi Wan), and even the funny-looking, wrinkly Alice the maid type (Yoda)! So we decided to kick off this special section of six *Star Wars* articles with a theme song borrowed (well, okay, stolen) from that other bunch! Sing along as we introduce...

"FILK"-ING THE FORCE

In fan parlance these kind of song parodies are known as "filks" and, according to Lucasfilm Internet content manager Pablo Hidalgo, there are countless fan-generated *Star Wars* filks to be found online if you do a quick search for them.

(SUNG TO THE TUNE OF...GOOD LORD, DO WE *REALLY* HAVE TO TELL YOU?)

Here's the story,
Of a sexy girl queen,
Living in a galaxy
   far, far away
When she was almost
   killed by rival forces
She knew she
   couldn't stay

Here's the story,
Of a young Skywalker
Who was learn-ing The
   Force both night and day
Taught by three Knights,
   playing with Light Sabers
It all seemed kind of gay

Then the people and their
   robots and the muppet
Got together and decided
   over brunch
That this group, must
   somehow fight the Dark Side
That's the way they all
   became the Jedi Bunch,

The Jedi Bunch -
   (You'll lose your lunch!)
That's the way -
   they became
   the Jedi Bunch!

ARTIST: SAM SISCO   WRITER: CHARLIE KADAU

MAD #419, July 2002
"The Jedi Bunch"

When *Star Wars Episode I* concluded, Anakin Skywalker was a precocious nine-year-old boy. When we meet him again in *Episode II*, he's already 19! It seems that George Lucas would just like to zip right past what, if he's anything like us, are the most difficult and awkward years in Anakin's life. The years when he's no longer a boy, yet not quite a man. The years of inner turmoil, confusion and, not to mention, (GAK!) puberty. Yeah, Lucas may have skipped over them, but WE won't! Join us as we pay a visit to...

ANAKIN SKYWALKER
THE HIGH SCHOOL YEARS

Anakin, how many times have I told you I don't like you wasting the entire day playing video games!

But these games are great! I can stage huge battles, race pods, fly spaceships, duel in hand-to-hand combat, even kill innocent people senselessly, without any consequences!

Indeed! I'm worried about the long-term effects that constantly playing these games will have on you! Games like these can foster all kinds of dangerously violent, antisocial tendencies!

Gimme a break! It's not like a little video game's gonna make me want to murder an entire planet or something!

ARTIST: MORT DRUCKER   WRITER: KENNY BYERLY

MAD #419, July 2002
"Anakin Skywalker: The High School Years"

"I DON'T LIKE YOU WASTING THE ENTIRE DAY PLAYING VIDEO GAMES!"

According to Daniel Logan (young Boba Fett in *Attack of the Clones*), one day on set in Australia between takes, Hayden Christensen invited Daniel to his dressing room, where he presented him with his Sony PlayStation. When Daniel asked why he was giving his PlayStation away, Hayden explained that he had just gotten a new Sega Dreamcast. Hayden then attached an outlet adaptor to his Dreamcast to fit into the Australian outlet and plugged it in, unfortunately forgetting that he also needed a voltage adaptor. The new Dreamcast immediately sparked, made a popping sound, and started to smoke. Daniel jokes that perhaps it was Sith lightning that caused the spark!

MORE CONDOM STORIES

According to Steve Sansweet, Lucasfilm director of content management and fan relations, in Japan there were actually counterfeit *Star Wars* condoms, called, for some reason, "Episode 7 Pieces," complete with a faux R2-D2 and C-3PO on the packaging. *MAD* wonders why they couldn't come up with a better name, like "Episode Sex—The Flaccid Menace," "Trojan Solo," "Ribbed Fortuna," or "The Rubber Alliance."

Counterfeit *Star Wars* condoms (not that there were ever any real *Star Wars* condoms).
Photo by Anne Neumann.
Courtesy of the Steve Sansweet collection.

There's a famous saying that goes something like, "Those who fail to learn from history are doomed to repeat it." Well, we couldn't help but notice that a long time ago, in a galaxy far, far away, a lot of things happened that are awfully similar to what's going on now in the "war on terror." Okay, we'll admit that the *Star Wars* series is actually fictional, but still — some of the parallels are more frightening than Jake Lloyd's performance as Anakin in *The Phantom Menace*! Don't believe us? Then check out these...

STARTLI

Use the Force, Anakin!

Obi-Wan Kenobi trained Anakin Skywalker, only to watch Anakin turn against him...

Use the rocket launcher, Osama!

...the CIA trained Osama bin Laden.

WHERE'S GERALDO?

You may have noticed that Geraldo also appeared in "The 21 Hottest Internet Rumors Regarding *Star Wars* Episode II: *Attack of the Clones*." That's because Geraldo was a favorite *MAD* punching bag for a while. At the time of this writing, it's Ann Coulter.

Thissa Gungan game Jar Jar like to call "Keeps away fromsa Jedis"!

Jar-Jar Binks is extremely annoying and somehow always makes himself the center of attention...

I'm here at the most **dangerous** location in all of Afghanistan, making such a **brave** and **heroic** sacrifice for the sake of you, my **loyal** viewers!

...Geraldo Rivera insisted on covering the war in Afghanistan.

The Force is a powerful ally!

Luke Skywalker is advised by Obi-Wan Kenobi, who is dead...

Dangerous and disturbing, this **puzzle** is. Begun, this **Clone** War has.

Yoda speaks in strange sentence patterns that are difficult to understand...

The **true** threat is whether or not one of these people decide, **peak** of anger, try to **hold** us hostage, ourselves; the Israelis, for example, to whom we'll **defend**, offer our **defenses**; the South Koreans.*

*Actual George W. Bush quote, Washington DC, March 13, 2001

...ditto President Bush.

Star Wars characters include several freakish-looking villains like Greedo and Jabba the Hutt...

ARTIST: HERMANN MEJIA   WRITER: GREG LEITMAN

MAD #419, July 2002
"Startling Similarities Between *Star Wars* and the War on Terrorism"

NG SIMILARITIES
BETWEEN
STAR WARS AND THE WAR ON TERRORISM

Civil liberties threaten our freedom!

... President Bush is advised by Attorney General John Ashcroft, who many believe is brain dead.

We are **not** warriors, we are **keepers** of the peace!

Mace Windu is a minority on the Jedi Council, wielding no real power but trying in vain to negotiate peaceful resolutions to the galaxy's bitter conflicts...

We don't have enough **support** in the Middle East to **attack** Iraq! Mr. President? Are you even listening to me?!

...Colin Powell functions in pretty much the same way for the Bush Administration.

Just look at all the **destruction** we're wreaking!

Where? I can't see!

Somebody give me a boost!

...Osama bin Laden's allies include the one-eyed Mullah Omar and a legless Saudi Sheik.

AAAWWRRRHH!

When he's in trouble, Chewbacca pounds on his chest and howls at his opposition...

Dammit, I'm **not** going to **answer** that **question**! Don't make me kick your bleeding heart liberal ass!

...When asked tough questions during press conferences, Secretary of Defense Rumsfeld behaves in a similar manner.

HEY LUCAS OVER DEPT.

In *Star Wars Episode I*, George Lucas included E.T. in the Republic Senate scene as a tip of the hat to his compadre Steven Speilberg. Next, the princes of pop, 'N Sync, almost managed to worm their way into *Star Wars Episode II*! But that's just the tip of the iceberg, as we found out when we took a close, close look at...

WHO'S IN THE CROWD IN

Howard the Duck
A bitter Lucas still harbors fantasies of turning this ill-conceived character into a Saturday morning cartoon.

Roger Ebert
Surprisingly, Ebert chose this bit part in the movie over a dozen Krispy Kreme donuts in exchange for a "thumbs up" review.

Dick Cheney
Desperate to line up any nation's support for an attack on Iraq.

Jaws
Lucas is paying off a Super Bowl bet to his buddy Speilberg by including the famous Great White in this scene.

The corpse of Alec Guinness
Hey, who cares if he's dead. In Hollywood, a contract is a contract.

Marlon Brando
Agreed to appear for free because he liked the artistic challenge of playing Jabba the Hutt's senator twin brother.

Anthony (George Lucas' Gardener)
For this, George gets 20% off next year's "edging and mowing" bill.

William Shatner
Confused actor showed up on set, Lucas felt sorry for him and let him stay.

Michelin Man, Pillsbury Doughboy, M&M, Ronald McDonald
Visiting senators from Planet Product-Placement.

Bill Clinton and Monica Lewinsky.

MAD #419, July 2002
"Who's in the Crowd in the New *Star Wars* Senate Scene"

THE NEW STAR WARS SENATE SCENE

ARTIST: ANGELO TORRES

WRITERS: DAN LEVINE AND MIKE MARTONE

Halle Berry
There to make sure "the door" doesn't close again on women of color, even if that color is green, blue or lavender.

Carrot Top
Lucas hired him because he looks like a space alien without the need for makeup.

Ted Koppel
Exploring a movie career now that it's all but certain he'll soon be out on his ass at ABC.

Millionaire Dennis Tito
Last year he paid his way onto the International Space Station. Now, a few million to Lucas buys him this.

Waldo
Hey, we found him! We found him!

The View's Star Jones
Making a guest cameo as Jabba the Hutt's senator twin sister.

Celine Dion
Admitted by Senate security who mistakenly mistook her for Jar Jar Binks.

Ron Popeil
There to peddle his GL7 spray-on hair, thinks it will be huge with balding Wookiees.

Attorney General John Ashcroft
His penchant for profiling aliens has really gotten out of control.

Katherine Harris
Lucas wrote her in to give credibility to the film's "Imperial election was fixed" subplot.

LIKE C-SPAN IN OUTER SPACE
In the actual films, Lucas gave characters names such as Nute Gunray and Lott Dod. Coincidence or not, if you followed American politics at all at the time, these names sounded a bit familiar.

home | my ecchbay | site map | sign in

Browse | Sell | Services | Search | Help | Community

item view

Attack of the Clones — AMAZING LOT— Script, Props + MORE!!!!!!!!!
Item # 1237645669

Film:Science Fiction:Star Wars:AOTC:Memorabilia:Worthless Crap

Currently	**$1,573.56**	First bid	**$100.00**
Quantity	**1**	# of bids	**34** bid history
Location	**Skywalker Ranch**	Country/Region	**USA/Marin County**

The Spiel

Seller (Rating) **Shady_Lucasfilm_Warehouse_Employee (2)**
view lame *Star Wars* quotes and references left by other fanatical losers in seller's
Feedback Profile | view seller's other contraband | use Jedi Mind Trick to convince seller
to end auction early and sell item to you for pennies on the dollar

Bid!

**Ruin the Good
Name Of...
(the seller)
(the sucker)**

High Bid	**Obsessing*On*Kenobi (37)**
Payment	Money Order/Cashiers Checks. Personal Checks. Spice. New Republic Credits. Will Not Accept Imperial Credits. Barter Okay.
Shipping	Buyer pays fixed shipping charges. Seller ships to United States, Canada, England, Tattooine, Naboo, Endor, and Alderaan. Shipping to smaller moons okay; contact seller with coordinates. Extra charge for overnight or hyperdrive shipping. Smuggler's insurance optional.
Miscellaneous	Must have a feedback rating of at least 25 to bid. Will not accept bids from: those with more than 5 negative feedback comments, bidders who have changed user names within last 30 days, or Jawas.

Mmm! Assumes all responsibility for listing item, seller does. Mmph! Contact seller to resolve questions before bidding,
you should. Ask....or ask not. There is no refund.

Description

Here's an out-of-this-world lot of original *Star Wars: Attack of the Clones* ephemera Anakin Skywalker would give his right hand for! Props and other such materials used in the production of *Star Wars* films are rarely made available to the public (at least legally), so that's all the more reason to bid now and bid high and hope you win, pay, and can take possession of these items before a power even greater than the Force steps in and shuts this auction down—the Lucasfilm Legal Department! Lot includes:

•A fascinating shooting script of the new film featuring many scenes ultimately deleted from the final version and therefore conveniently not subject to any sort of verification. Script pages are littered with indecipherable scribbled notes and doodles in the margins, unattached to one another, and in complete random order in an effort to best emulate the particularly over-complicated, disjointed, confusing feel of this latest entry in the *Star Wars* canon of feature films.

•One full quart (32 ounces) of Kenny Baker's sweat collected from the bottom of R2-D2 after a day of shooting in Tunisia.

•Sixty-eight pounds of prop Bantha dung made from a mixture of elephant manure and lasagna noodles seen (blurred) in a quick pan of the Tusken Raider village during Sc. 322-A.

•RARE! An INCREDIBLE FULL SET of Clone Trading Cards. Each card in this pre-production run features a close-up color photo of every clone that appears in *Star Wars Episode II: Attack of the Clones!* The manufacturer later cancelled production when research showed that there was little interest, even in the most obsessed, die-hard *Star Wars* fans, of collecting 10,000 identical trading cards.

All items to be shipped securely in cushioning materials composed of shredded first draft copies of the script that featured Jar Jar Binks in a more substantial role.

ARTIST: SCOTT BRICHER **WRITER: SCOTT MAIKO**

EBAY OUTWEIRDS *MAD*

As outlandish as the stuff *MAD* made up for this eBay parody might be, truth has proven to be stranger than fiction. Lucasfilm staffer Dennis vonGalle, for example, purchased a split hambone on eBay that looks like Darth Vader's mask.

Darth Hambone.
Courtesy of Dennis vonGalle.

MAD #419, July 2002
"*MAD*'s Ecchbay Item of the Month: *Attack of the Clones*"

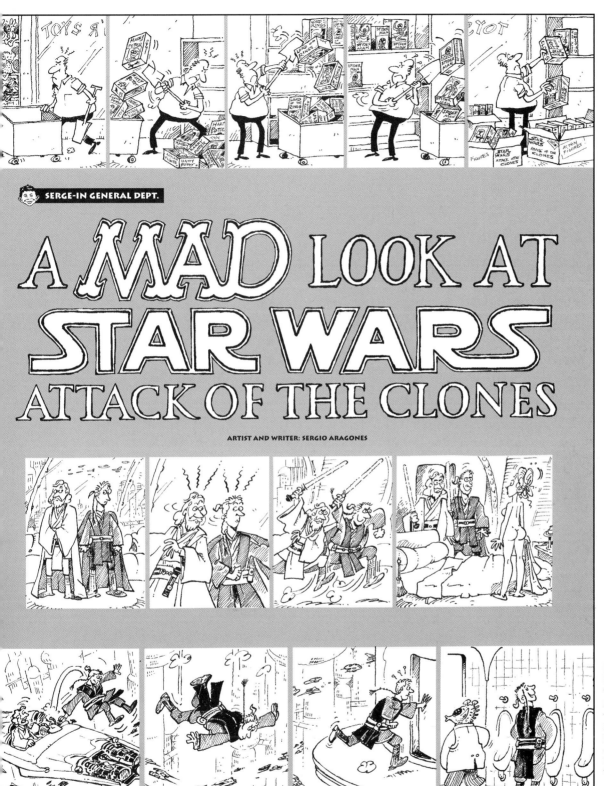

SERGE-IN GENERAL DEPT.

A *MAD* LOOK AT
STAR WARS
ATTACK OF THE CLONES

ARTIST AND WRITER: SERGIO ARAGONÉS

**LIKE FATHER,
LIKE SON**
This gag here where Anakin
Skywalker makes a run for
the bathroom is a bit of an
homage to the famous Luke-
in-the-bathroom gag Aragonés
did for the original "A *MAD*
Look at '*Star Wars*,'" seen in
this book on page 10.

MAD #421, September 2002
"A *MAD* Look at *Star Wars: Attack of the Clones*"

CHECK OUT WHO'S AT THE BAR

Sergio Aragonés likes to hide people in his gags. Notice, for example, in the third panel of this gag is a certain bearded fellow in a flannel shirt. Standing behind him in a Hawaiian shirt is cartoonist Scott Shaw, of Captain Carrot fame. Aragonés frequently hides him in his gags. In panel two, check out Marge Simpson on the left side of the frame.

OBI-WAN'S SHRINKING CLOAK

According to costume designer Trisha Biggar, Obi-Wan's wool cloak would literally shrink before everyone's eyes when it got wet, and several cloaks had to be used to get through the scene. There's a life lesson here for anyone who's ever considered buying a T-shirt from a street vendor in New York City.

YODA HAS A HEART ATTACK

Because Yoda was created digitally in Episode II, Frank Oz was spared from having to puppeteer the fight scenes. Even so, given Yoda's age, Oz felt that perhaps the battle in Episode II should have ended a bit more like the way Aragonés depicted it here.

JEDI IN DISGUISE

At *Star Wars* Celebration II, Hayden Christensen and his brother, Tove, wanted to roam the convention floor, but couldn't for fear of getting mobbed. So they donned a couple of stormtrooper helmets and went about unmolested. Think about that, autograph hounds, next time you are at a convention. The "geek" in the costume next to you could be a movie star. (Pull the mask off at your own risk, though. The security detail is probably those guys in the Wookiee suits.)

MAD #454, June 2005
"Monroe and *Star Wars*"

FAKE AUTOGRAPHS

Apparently there are a lot of forgeries of Mark Hamill's and Anthony Daniels's autographs out there. Unfortunately, at the time of this writing, Mark Hamill actually signed the warning he posted on his website, making it that much easier to get hold of a copy of his signature to forge. (Unless, of course, it's a fake signature that he posted so he can trap would-be forgers. Hmmm.)

SPY VADER SPY

SPY VS. SPY MEETS THE DARK SIDE

At *Star Wars* Celebration IV, a giant *Star Wars* convention held in LA during Memorial Day Weekend 2007 to celebrate the 30th Anniversary of *Star Wars*, fans were treated to the world premiere exhibition of The Vader Project. Presented by Master Replicas, Inc., and curated by Dov Kelemer of DKE Toys, sixty-six hot underground and pop surrealist painters, artists, and designers were given full-scale replicas of Darth Vader's helmet and free reign to customize them as they saw fit. One of the artists was *MAD*'s own Peter Kuper. Kuper was inspired by the angular lines on the sides of the mask which come to a point on either side of Vader's chin. Kuper thought that they matched the Spies beak-like faces perfectly, and soon created the Spy Vs. Spy masterpiece seen here.

From The Vader Project, *Star Wars* Celebration IV, May 24 to May 28, 2007.
Helmet design by Peter Kuper. Darth Vader helmet prop replica by Master Replicas, Inc.
Photos by Justin Lubin. Courtesy of DKE Toys.

JEDI KNIGHTMARE DEPT.

There is unrest in the movie theaters. Several thousand multiplexes, under the leadership of George Lucas, are foisting more stiff acting, droid-like dialogue and convoluted plotlines upon a weary and disgusted public. This unfortunate development has made it difficult for the extremely limited number of remaining fans to maintain interest in...

STAR BORES

I'm **Oldie Von Moldie**, Jet-eye master! There is great unrest in the **Galactic Senate**! So what else is **new**? Hell, the day the **unrest stops**, this **endless parade** of mind-numbing *Star Bores* adventures will end and my **confusing** life will **finally** be **over**! I mean, I **started out** as an **old man**, then I **died**, then I was **young again**! Now I'm **aging** all over **again**! No one ever **knows** how many **candles** to put on my **birthday cake**! The only **good news** is that I'm **young again**, but because of a **book-keeping** error I **still** collect my **Senior Jet-eye pension**!

I'm **Mannequin Skystalker**, apprentice to **Oldie Von Moldie**! I was an **apprentice** in the **last** *Star Bores* movie, and I'm **still** an **apprentice**! Jet-eye knights may have **hi-tech** equipment, but what we **really** need is a **strong union** to **fight** for **quicker advancement**! Then again, it **might** be my **rebellious attitude**! Jet-eye law **forbids** romantic **attachments**, but **Senator AmaDilly** and I have been **practicing docking maneuvers**! I'm **not worried**, though! **Now** that she's a **politician**, if **anyone** asks, AmaDilly automatically says, "I **did not** have **sex** with that **Jet-eye**, Mr. Skystalker"!

I'm **Senator PetMe AmaDilly**, the former Queen of **No-boo-boo** and current **Skystalker heartthrob**! I've **joined** the **Galactic Senate** to **vote** on the **critical issue** of **creating** an **Army** of the **Republic** to **assist** the overwhelmed **Jet-eye knights**! I'm **also** pushing a **vote** for **women** to get some **easier-to-take-care-of hairstyles**! These **ridiculous** do's take **hours** a day to **wash, set and blow-dry**!

"SUICIDE" COSTUMES

According to concept designer Iain McCaig, he purposely tried designing hairstyles that Lucas would reject, but Lucas never did. McCaig called this design the "suicide costume," since Natalie Portman would likely end up killing herself trying to walk through a doorway with it, or turning her head too fast, causing her noggin to corkscrew off.

A "suicide" costume.
Photo by Jay Maidment.
© Lucasfilm Ltd. & TM. All rights reserved.

Meesa is **Har Har Blinks**! It'sa **amazin'** howsa many peoples **hates** meesa! Wella **MADsa** gonna do **youse** a favor **George Lucasa** nevers do! **Thisa** is only time yousa see **meesa**! Yousa can say **thanksa** to MAD **bysa** subscribing at **madmag.com**! Tell them **Har Har sentsa yousa**!

Master Yodel am **I**! Dispensing **wise sayings** have been **doing I forever**! "**May the Force Be With You**" from my **mind** has **come**! Okay, so **originally** I said maybe: "**With you, may the force be**," but basically **still** my **idea** it is! I **talk** always **asteroid backwards**!

I'm **Bar Stool**, sometimes known as **R2D2**! I just **heard** some **bad news**! Now **there's** a **newer** model **Astromech Droid**, **R4D4**, which is **much more powerful** than me! **Hoo boy**! Now I **know** how the **Sega System** felt when the **XBox** came **along**!

I'm **Damn Weasel**, bounty hunter! My **mission** is to **kill** Senator **AmaDilly**! This **vial** contains poisonous **Kewpies**! I plan to have my **droid** release these **creepy, crawling** things in her **bed**! Though, to be **honest**, I think **AmaDilly** is **much more** worried about **another insect** ruining her and everyone else's **summer** — **Spider-Man**!

MAD #421, September 2002
"Star Bores: Epic Load II Attack of the Clowns"

EPIC LOAD II
ATTACK OF THE CLOWNS

ARTIST: MORT DRUCKER   WRITER: DICK DEBARTOLO

I'm **Lace Windows, senior member** of the **High Council!** I'm **quite concerned** by the **growing disturbance** in the **Force!** I'm even **more concerned** that **all I ever get to do** in **any** of these movies is, well, **look concerned!** In the **last** *Star Bores* movie I just **looked plain old concerned**, but in **this movie**, it's a **much more demanding role**, so you'll **see me** look *deeply* concerned!

I'm **Chancellor Palpitation, head** of the **Senate!** I have to be **very careful** that **anything** I **say** or **do** doesn't **cause an all-out war** with the **Separatwits!** The **Separatwits** have the **ability** to **produce millions** of clones **ready** to do their **bidding** — sort of like **Scientologists**, but **less scary!**

I am **Count Cuckoo, leader** of the **Separatwits!** Even though I'm **getting on** in **years** and I **can't get** my **light saber** to **work** like I used to **without special effects** — mainly **Viagra** — I'm **still** a **sharp adversary** to be **contended** with! And as **soon as** I **remember** exactly **who** my **adversary** is, he better **watch out!** Now **where did** I **put** the **keys** to my **Solar Sailer?** And **where did** I **put** my **Solar Sailer?** And **do I need** keys?

"I CAN'T GET MY LIGHT SABER TO WORK LIKE I USED TO..."
Yet another suggestive light-saber gag. And don't worry, you'll see it again before you finish reading this book!

I'm **Kid Twisto, Jet-eye Master!** I'm in **this film** not **because** the **Republic** needed my **help**, but because **Hasbro** did! They needed **one more action figure** to **round out** their *Star Bores* toy line!

I'm **Tango Feet**, the **bounty hunter** chosen to be the **template** for the **Army of Clones** that will **battle** the **Federation!** Each **clone** will have **all my** traits: my **genius-like intelligence**, my **superhuman physical strength**, my **superior cunning** and **agility**, and **most of all**, my **sense** of **modesty!** Oh, there's **one other thing** all the clones **share** with **me**: absolutely **no acting ability whatsoever!**

Hey George! **Alf** here! **Why** don't **I** have a **part** in this **film?** You want a **weird looking alien?** I am a **weird looking alien!** You want **attitude?** I **reek attitude!** You want something that's **100% owned** and **merchandised** by **Lucas, Inc.?** Oh, **that's why** I'm **not** in **this film!** Ha!

I'm **George Lucas**, and **I'm sick** of the **critics** saying that my *Star Bores* movies are **lackluster** and **repetitive!** I'd **like** to **see anyone** of them **write** the **same** movie **nine times** and **make it appear fresh!**

"BLUE MOONS"

MAD used the euphemism "Blue Moons" here because the editors didn't have the stones to use the real phrase.

I finally caught you, Damn Weasel! Now **tell** me, who hired you?

It was a **bounty hunter** called Ga-Ga-Gasp!

Hmm… Ga-Ga-Gasp? That name doesn't ring a bell!

It's **not** a name! That was my dying breath, idiot! Ciao!

Now we're at a dead end!

To NoBooBoo, out of harm's way, Senator AmaDilly, Mannequin takes! Makes no sense, did that, to me, even!

Oldie Von Moldie is too **critical** of me! I'm **far** more **advanced** than he **thinks** I am!

Manny, don't try to **grow up** too fast! And please don't look at me like that! I can see what you're **thinking!**

Really? Come a little closer and you just might **feel** what I'm **thinking!**

The **power** of the **Force** is **with you,** that's for sure!

"COME A LITTLE CLOSER AND YOU JUST MIGHT FEEL WHAT I'M THINKING!"
Check out the less-than-subtle visual gag with Anakin's light-saber hilt. Never let it be said that *MAD*'s illustrators, er, shrink at, um, augmenting the, uh, dictates of the script.

Meanwhile **Oldie, Trex,** he **does** find!

Can you tell me where this **poison** dart came from?

Can you **cross** my palm with **silver?**

No, but I can cross your **face** with my **fist!**

In **that** case, the dart is from the Planet **Kinko!** They're **cloners!** They love to **copy** things! They **make** clones 24/7!

"Here's the **forecast** for **Kinko!** Showers for the next 2,000 **Shanigans,** followed by **heavy rain,** followed by **thunderstorms!** The **weather** will **turn inclement** after **that!**"

We made 200,000 **clone soldiers!** As soon as we **install** the 400,000 **AA batteries,** they'll be **ready** for battle!

They're **cloned** from **me,** Tango Feet!

I see that! It **would** be nice if you had **stood** up a little **straighter** before they **cloned** you! Now we have 200,000 clones with **extremely** bad posture!

Meanwhile, **Mannequin** on a **quest** for his **mother,** to **Spittooine,** he does **go!** Big help, **Whatzzup,** will be!

You think **finding** your **mother** will **really end** those **years** of sleepless-ness, Manny?

I'm **positive** it will! She **has** a **prescription** to help me sleep!

Pills?

No, she has a **copy** of this **screenplay!** I'll **go** right out!

Let's hope Oldie isn't **furious** because you **disobeyed** his **orders** by **leaving** NoBooBoo!

We have **MegaMotorola Transponders** to keep in **touch** with each other! Of course, when I'm **this far away,** I shut mine off in order to avoid the **intergalactic roaming charges!**

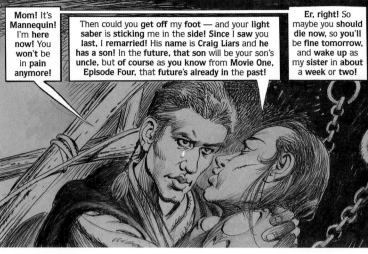

PADMÉ AMIDALA'S SODA CANS

While *MAD*'s version of Padmé Amidala appears to have a fondness for Diet Coke, Lucasfilm had actually given Pepsi the license to put her likeness all over soda cans.

Pepsi Amidala.
Courtesy of the Duncan Jenkins collection.
© Lucasfilm Ltd. & TM. All rights reserved.

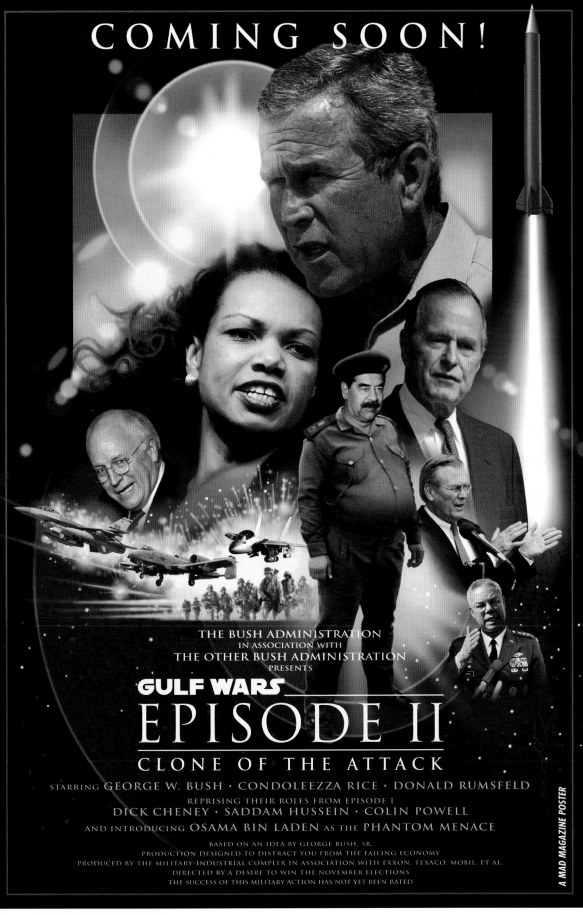

COMING SOON!

THE BUSH ADMINISTRATION
IN ASSOCIATION WITH
THE OTHER BUSH ADMINISTRATION
PRESENTS

GULF WARS
EPISODE II
CLONE OF THE ATTACK

STARRING GEORGE W. BUSH · CONDOLEEZZA RICE · DONALD RUMSFELD
REPRISING THEIR ROLES FROM EPISODE I
DICK CHENEY · SADDAM HUSSEIN · COLIN POWELL
AND INTRODUCING OSAMA BIN LADEN AS THE PHANTOM MENACE

BASED ON AN IDEA BY GEORGE BUSH, SR.
PRODUCTION DESIGNED TO DISTRACT YOU FROM THE FAILING ECONOMY
PRODUCED BY THE MILITARY-INDUSTRIAL COMPLEX IN ASSOCIATION WITH EXXON, TEXACO, MOBIL, ET AL.
DIRECTED BY A DESIRE TO WIN THE NOVEMBER ELECTIONS
THE SUCCESS OF THIS MILITARY ACTION HAS NOT YET BEEN RATED

A MAD MAGAZINE POSTER

BUSH LOVED THIS (UNFORTUNATELY)

MAD editor-in-chief John Ficarra reports that a member of the White House press corps gave a copy of this issue to then-press secretary Ari Fleischer, who passed it on to President Bush. Word soon came down that this parody was a huge hit in the Oval Office—much to *MAD*'s dismay. In fact, *MAD* got requests to provide issues for Donald Rumsfeld and Condoleezza Rice.

Not only did it have fans in the Bush administration, but to put salt in the wound, Fox News loved it as well. According to the coauthor of this piece, Arie Kaplan (brother, coincidentally of Lucasfilm Animation character modeler David Kaplan), it was so popular that it even made it onto Fox News' *Special Report with Brit Hume* on March 19, 2003. Hume apparently first tells the viewer that the U.S. military has been dropping leaflets and transmitting radio broadcasts urging Iraqis to surrender. He then states that "they're even showing a major motion picture across Iraq at secret screening locations across Iraq. And we have obtained a key piece of promotion for that film."

This *MAD* poster parody was then shown on screen.

Apparently Brit didn't get that the Bush administration was the butt of the joke. Humor just doesn't seem to be something Fox News understands, as *The 1/2 Hour News Hour* so aptly demonstrates.

The only consolation in all this was that the poster was a hit on the Internet, and was also well-received by the *Star Wars* crew. In fact, Episode II screenwriter Jonathan Hales commented that "we were e-mailing it all about."

MAD #424, December 2002
"Gulf Wars: Episode II Clone of the Attack"
(Writers: Arie Kaplan and Scott Sonneborn; Artist: Scott Bricher; Photos: AP/WorldWide Photos)

MAY THE FA FA FA BE WITH YOU!

Here I am writing you from the valley of the insane, but with good reason. Today, I happened to buy issue #454 and noticed this horrific horrible flaw that should be punishable by death. On your cover you have Anakin Skywalker and Obi-Wan fighting with red sabers! When in reality they have blue sabers. Wan has always had a blue saber and Ani only gets a red saber after he's burnt to a crisp. I know you are probably very sorry and because most generous am I, I have decided to forgive you.

Tazara Dorsey,
Tallahassee, FL

Use the Dorse — You call yourself a *Star Wars* fan? We're surprised you didn't know that even as we write this, George "I'm going to ring every penny out of this franchise" Lucas is re-mastering *Revenge of the Sith* and changing the colors of all the light sabers to red. Other changes include: C-3PO now speaks with a thick Spanish accent, Emperor Palpatine has Elvis-style mutton chops and Mace Windu is now a white woman! Check back in a month for news on Lucas' *special* special edition that will further revise this special edition! —Ed.

Letters page excerpt from *MAD* #457, September 2005.

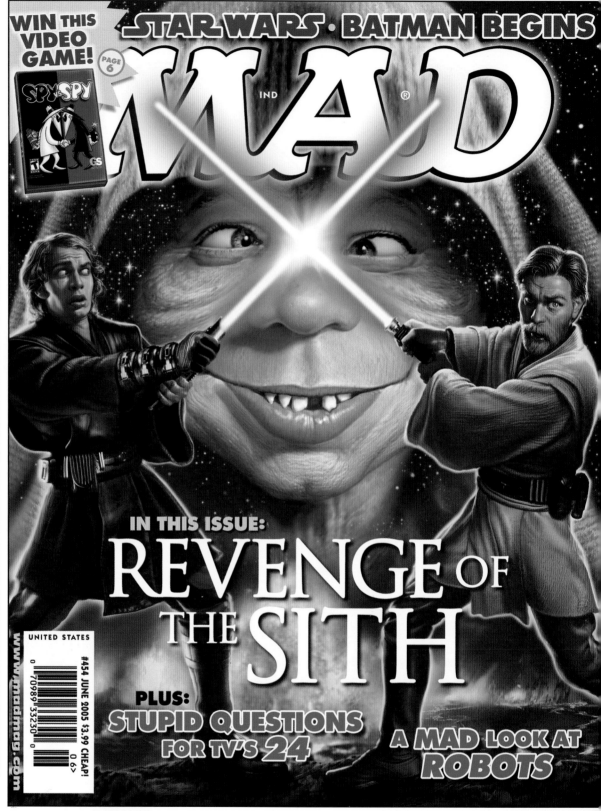

MAD #454, June 2005
Cover, Alfred as Emperor Palpatine
(Artist: Mark Fredrickson)

Star Wars: Episode III – REVENGE OF THE SITH
Opening Crawl: The Annotated Edition

Good God, y'all! What is it good for? Absolutely profit!

Just like this whole tired franchise.

War! The Republic is crumbling under attacks by the ruthless Sith Lord, Count Dooku. There are heroes on both sides. Evil is everywhere.

Hmm... "Dooku for Cocoa Puffs." How did George's licensing vipers miss making a deal on that product tie-in?

Call us crazy, but how the hell can those who work for a "ruthless Sith Lord" be called "heroes"?

How fiendish? Check out this name!

In a stunning move, the fiendish droid leader, General Grievous, has swept into the Republic capital and kidnapped Chancellor Palpatine, leader of the Galactic Senate.

Ugh, this is starting to read like Bush's State of the Union Address. What next, will they try to link Vader to 9/11?

What, was "Hitler von Killington" too subtle? How about "Sergeant Satanstein"?

His plans to kidnap Letterman's son were foiled.

Probably comprised of droid reservists who had no idea what they were getting into when they signed up.

As the Separatist Droid Army attempts to flee the besieged capital with their valuable hostage, two Jedi Knights lead a desperate mission to rescue the captive Chancellor...

Spoiler alert: it's not Yaddle and Kit Fisto!

If it's such a "desperate" mission, why'd they only send two Jedis, one of whom is a nutjob with an insatiable thirst for slaughtering Sand People?

"HITLER VON KILLINGTON"

Since Lucas tends to use none-too-subtle names for his villains (Tyranus, Grievous, Maul, et al.), *MAD* is kind of hoping that he might actually go for "Hitler von Killington" when it comes to his new television series.

MAD #454, June 2005
"*Star Wars: Episode III—Revenge of the Sith* Opening Crawl: The Annotated Edition"

STAR BORE DEPT.

Don't let the 15-year gap between movies fool you — George Lucas is a busy, busy man! Why, between making one of the most beloved movie series of all time, ruining that series, AND trying to save that series, he's got quite a full plate! Just take a look at...

A DAY IN THE LIFE OF

C-3POS CEREAL

C-3POs was an actual cereal that came out in 1984. They were "twin rings of honey sweetened oats, corn and wheat, fused together in outer space for a truly galactic breakfast." When Anthony Daniels had to do the television commercials for them, however, he thought that the "twin rings" looked like the number eight, and started referring to them as C-3P8s. The producers were not thrilled with this and made him eat an entire box—a rather extreme punishment, as Daniels considered the cereal to be inedible.

Should you be dying to see what the back of a box of C-3POs looks like, here I am at an ILM Halloween party in the C-3POs costume I made using the Lucasfilm library's color copier. My costume was well received until the librarians got to work the following Monday and it was discovered that I had neglected to tell anyone that I had burned out the expensive, high-end copier in the process of making my costume.

Me in my C-3POs box.
Photo by Halina Krukowski.
© Lucasfilm Ltd. & TM. All rights reserved.

7:30 A.M. P.M.

Start the day with a nice big bowl of slightly stale C-3PO's from 1984!

8:42 A.M. P.M.

9:26 A.M. P.M.

See what Ziggy's up to today.

10:19 A.M. P.M.

Call digital imaging crew and order new footage added to cantina scene so it's now absolutely, positively clear that Greedo shot first.

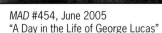

MAD #454, June 2005
"A Day in the Life of George Lucas"

GEORGE LUCAS

7:55 A.M. P.M.

Get things moving with a nice hot cup of coffee and then head off to the bathroom to drop some rebels into the ol' sarlacc pit.

8:12 A.M. P.M.

What to wear, what to wear?

Put idle Industrial Light & Magic crew to work replacing that burned-out bulb on the patio.

9:58 A.M. P.M.

Principal photography has started on Star Wars VII, which takes place twelve years after The Return of the Jedi, on the candy planet Wonkaraan. Five lucky young Padawans, who have each found a golden_

Start random, completely untrue *Star Wars* rumors on the internet, under a phony screen name, just for the hell of it.

12:00 A.M. P.M.

Lunch at the Bearded Directors Club.

1:48 A.M. P.M.

Meet with John Williams to discuss composing score for the ranch's new doorbell.

ARTIST: HERMANN MEJIA   WRITER: SCOTT MAIKO

GEORGE LUCAS WASN'T THRILLED WITH THESE CARICATURES

When I spoke to George Lucas at the "Dressing a Galaxy" *Star Wars* fashion show in the fall of 2005, he let me know that as much as he still loved *MAD* Magazine, he preferred the way Mort Drucker caricatured him to the more severe version by Hermann Mejia seen here. I at first thought of telling him I would see what I could do—in exchange, of course, for him slipping me a few bucks—but then I remembered the mistake I had made my first week at Lucasfilm when I'd playfully threatened Lucas with a prop *Young Indiana Jones* rifle and demanded that a few changes in the salary structure at Skywalker Ranch be made. So, rather than opening my mouth, I just squirmed awkwardly.

IS "SCOTT MAIKO" A PSEUDONYM?

Soon after this issue hit the stands, I got calls from some of my former Lucasfilm colleagues, asking if I had written this under a pen name. To set the record straight, Scott Maiko, the author of this article, is indeed a real person. It was that same issue's "What Caused Anakin Skywalker to Become Darth Vader" (see page 134) that I wrote under a pen name.

A DAY IN THE LIFE OF GEORGE LUCAS

Cancel the additional footage. Let Han shoot first, who cares?

Do more harm than good while unsuccessfully trying to get out of a speeding ticket by using an old Jedi mind trick.

Feign amusement when car salesman makes lame joke that car "made the Kessel run in less than 12 parsecs."

On second thought, decide to put that shot of Greedo shooting first back in.

After mulling it over some more, ask digital imaging crew to try it with Greedo and Han shooting each other at the same time.

Approve a few new *Star Wars* licensees and products.

Smooth things over with cop by promising to digitally insert his face in a crowd scene in DVD release of *Revenge of the Sith*.

Meet with son's teacher to discuss the allegation that he may have had some outside help with his science project.

While napping, make another $180,000 in toy sales around the world.

Meet with kid who played Anakin in the first prequel; give him a summer job pulling weeds and picking up cigarette butts around Skywalker Ranch.

Play *KOTOR II* and spend four hours stuck in the Droid Warehouse on Nar Shadda trying to find the damn rotation code to open the door. Make a note to call that frickin' head programmer at LucasArts and find out how to advance, then fire him.

Issue final decision on Han and Greedo scene: Bro-Hug.

"WHILE NAPPING, MAKE ANOTHER $180,000"

In the early days, following the success of the first *Star Wars* movie, Lucasfilm was still depositing checks through a teller window at the local bank. Lucy Autrey Wilson, one of Lucasfilm's first employees, has many a story about making sure the wide-eyed tellers got the number of zeros right, and that, yes, those were checks for that many millions of dollars. Looking back now, Wilson realizes that since she had the authority to endorse and deposit all those checks, it's a good thing she was raised to be honest or she might have run off with the money to South America!

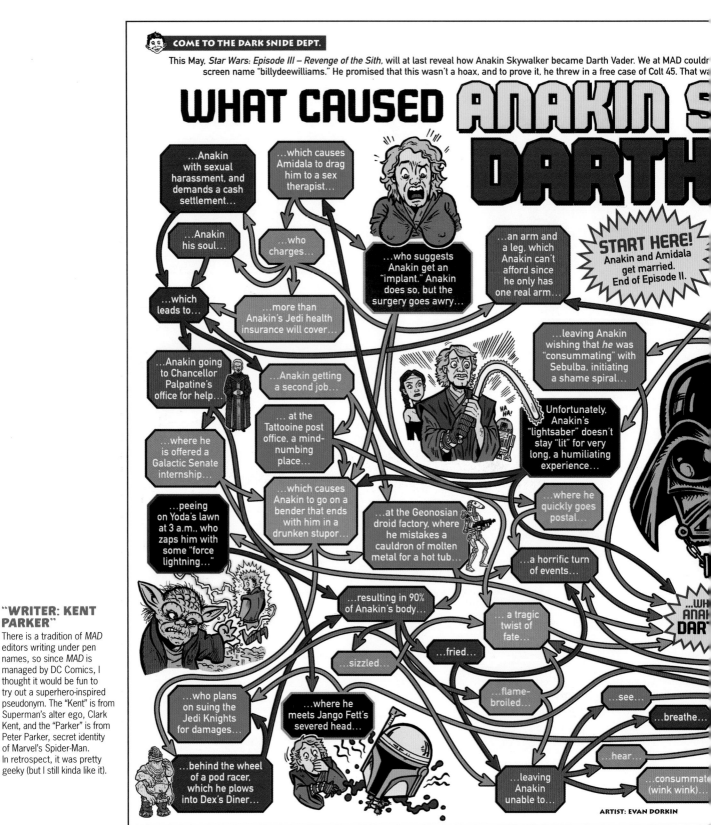

MAD #454, June 2005
"What Caused Anakin Skywalker to Become Darth Vader?"

"WRITER: KENT PARKER"

There is a tradition of MAD editors writing under pen names, so since MAD is managed by DC Comics, I thought it would be fun to try out a superhero-inspired pseudonym. The "Kent" is from Superman's alter ego, Clark Kent, and the "Parker" is from Peter Parker, secret identity of Marvel's Spider-Man. In retrospect, it was pretty geeky (but I still kinda like it).

wait, so we bought bootleg screenplay drafts from a cash-strapped, former Lucasfilm employee we met online who goes by the enigmatic proof enough for us! So, here, dear readers, is a flow chart summarizing all the plot points George Lucas considered as he decided...

KYWALKER TO BECOME VADER?

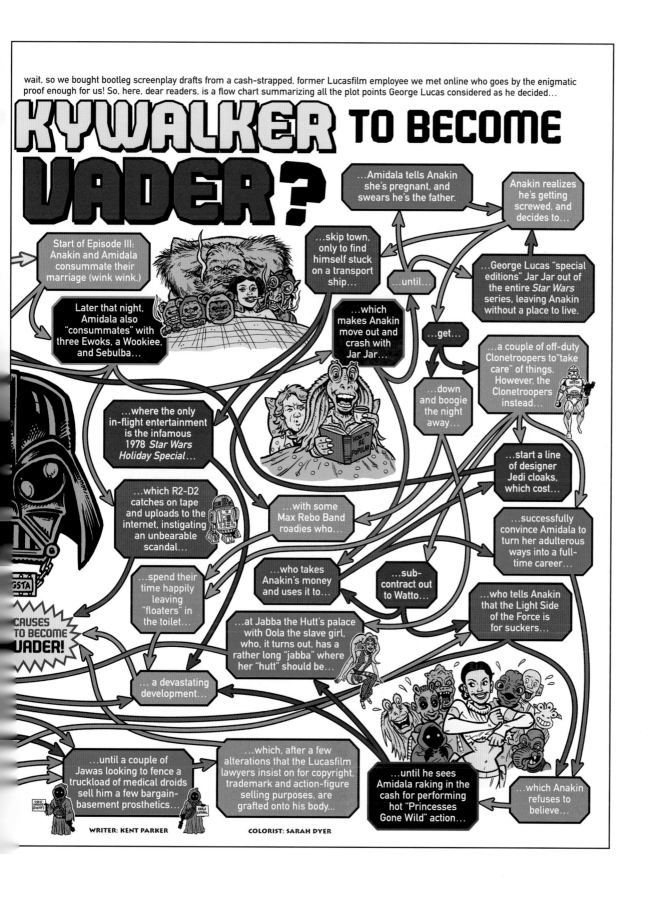

...Amidala tells Anakin she's pregnant, and swears he's the father.

Anakin realizes he's getting screwed, and decides to...

Start of Episode III: Anakin and Amidala consummate their marriage (wink wink.)

...skip town, only to find himself stuck on a transport ship...

...until...

...George Lucas "special editions" Jar Jar out of the entire *Star Wars* series, leaving Anakin without a place to live.

Later that night, Amidala also "consummates" with three Ewoks, a Wookiee, and Sebulba...

...which makes Anakin move out and crash with Jar Jar...

...get...

...a couple of off-duty Clonetroopers to "take care" of things. However, the Clonetroopers instead...

...where the only in-flight entertainment is the infamous 1978 *Star Wars* Holiday Special...

...down and boogie the night away...

...start a line of designer Jedi cloaks, which cost...

...which R2-D2 catches on tape and uploads to the internet, instigating an unbearable scandal...

...with some Max Rebo Band roadies who...

...successfully convince Amidala to turn her adulterous ways into a full-time career...

CAUSES TO BECOME VADER!

...spend their time happily leaving "floaters" in the toilet...

...who takes Anakin's money and uses it to...

...sub-contract out to Watto...

...who tells Anakin that the Light Side of the Force is for suckers...

...at Jabba the Hutt's palace with Oola the slave girl, who, it turns out, has a rather long "jabba" where her "hutt" should be...

... a devastating development...

...until a couple of Jawas looking to fence a truckload of medical droids sell him a few bargain-basement prosthetics...

...which, after a few alterations that the Lucasfilm lawyers insist on for copyright, trademark and action-figure selling purposes, are grafted onto his body...

...until he sees Amidala raking in the cash for performing hot "Princesses Gone Wild" action...

...which Anakin refuses to believe...

WRITER: KENT PARKER   COLORIST: SARAH DYER

"DROID SEEKING DROID"
According to Anthony Daniels, C-3PO doesn't really need another droid. Instead, he has a favorite electrical outlet he likes to plug into. It gives him a tingly feeling. (Eww.)

MAY THE FOR SALE BE WITH YOU DEPT.

IF THE STAR WARS GALAXY HAD CLASSIFIED ADS

The Tatooine Tribune

PERSONALS

Male Seeking Female

YOU were the gal wearing a sexy slave bikini around Jabba's palace. I was the fella who looks like a blue elephant playing the piano. I felt a disturbance in the Force when I saw you. Call me.
(Comlink Channel 4) Max Rebo

MESA WANSA BE HAVIN' A GOOD TIME!
Yousa gooooood-lookin' princess lookin' for de fun. Mesa 'gooooood-lookin' maxi big boss from Naboo w/de long tongue (if you knowsa what mesa be sayin'). Yousa come to mesa pad, where mesa love you long time.
Contact Supreme Chancellor Palpatine Comlink Channel 8839

Female Seeking Male

HELP ME, OBI-WAN KENOBI, YOU'RE MY ONLY HOPE!
General Kenobi, years ago you served my father in the Clone Wars. Now he begs you to help him in his struggle against the Empire. I regret that I am unable to present my father's request to you in person, but my ship has fallen under attack and I'm afraid my mission to bring you to Alderaan has failed. I have placed information vital to the survival of the Rebellion into the memory systems of this R2 unit. My father will know how to retrieve it. You must see this droid safely delivered to him on Alderaan. This is our most desperate hour. Help me, Obi-Wan Kenobi, you're my only hope. Call me – Leia – Comlink Channel 7008392

Droid Seeking Droid

ARE YOU THE DROID I'M LOOKING FOR?
Single, golden, protocol droid tired of human-cyborg relations, seeks short, dome-headed R2 unit on which to lavish loving abuse and motor oil. "Goldenrod," Comlink 1138

Droid Seeking Droid

BLOOP BLEEP BLOOT BLEEP?
Boop Boop Beep Deet Blat! Dirp Weeeee Ding Bweeee Blop? Be-doo, Bwip, Bop, Bloot, Candlelit dinners. Boop Beep Bop Ding Whoop Blot. R2-D2.
Comlink Channel 8675309

Misc.

SWC (Single White Clone) seeks same
Comlink Channel 8923

SWC (Single White Clone) seeks same
Comlink Channel 8924

SWC (Single White Clone) seeks same
Comlink Channel 8925

SWC (Single White Clone) seeks same
Comlink Channel 8926

You were the astromech droid in the speeder. I was the Jawa with lights in his eyes (literally). We passed at 774th floor of the Big Blue Building in Coruscant. Was there a spark? Or was that your restraining bolt? Let's find out. Comlink Channel 20939

LOST AND FOUND

LOST LIGHTSABER
Standard Jedi issue, blue blade. Still has my severed hand attached from when my dad "accidentally" chopped it off. Last seen falling down Cloud City exhaust shaft. If found, please call L. Skywalker (Comlink 72929)

REWARD!

HAVE YOU SEEN MY TAUNTAUN?
Missing since last Thursday on snowy plains of Hoth. Long snout. Lots of drool. House-broken, with Rebel saddle. Answers to the name "Barry."

REWARD!
Wedge Antilles, Comlink 293002

MERCHANDISE FOR SALE

Vehicles – New and Used

Why WALK the forest when you can ZIP through it? New SPEEDERBIKES at CLOSEOUT PRICES! FREE "Tree Dodging" Seminar w/every purchase ALL NAME BRANDS: Imperial, Rebel, Kawasaki

ENDOR SPEEDERBIKE LEASING AND SALES
Endor Freeway, just opposite Ewok Village

Misc.

HELMETS, HELMETS, HELMETS
Want to strike fear into the hearts of Rebel Scum? Worried your Imperial Wardrobe is missing that certain "some-thing"? Well, we've got just what you need — helmets! That's right! STORMTROOPER HELMETS! CLONE TROOPER HELMETS! BOBA FETT! JANGO FETT! GAMORREAN GUARDS! IMPERIAL GUARDS! TIE FIGHTER PILOTS and DEATH STAR GUNNERS! Even a couple of helmets custom-made for Vader himself! So come on down! We can custom color match your new helmet with your existing armor! Mention this ad!
THE IMPERIAL HELMET STATION
Comlink Channel 83936

BANTHAS, BANTHAS, BANTHAS
My bantha just gave birth to a litter of eight bantha pups and we are giving them away — free! Who wouldn't want these cuddly, 8-foot-tall horned omnivores? Their tendency to eat everything in sight makes them natural garbage disposals. The copious amounts of poodoo make great garden fertilizer, and the frequent scent-marking keeps pesky nunas away. Come by anytime. (Please!)
T. Usken Raider
Comlink Channel 288309

The Tatooine Tribune

EDUCATION

ALWAYS FALLING FOR THE JEDI MIND TRICK?
This is the mind training course you are looking for. You will send 50,000 credits to: Jedi Mind Tricks 837 Greedo Way Coruscant X82-87

LEARN THE WAYS OF THE FORCE – DARK & LIGHT
* Levitation * Mind Control * Object Throwing * Choking People Without Touching Them * Foreseeing the Future * Shooting Laser Bolts From Your Fingers *
IMPRESS YOUR FRIENDS! IMPRESS YOUR DATES! GREAT PARTY TRICKS!
For an application: www.ForceAcademy.emp

YOUSA NO SPEAK SO GOOD? SPEAK WELL, YOU DO NOT?
Whether yousa speaksa de Gungun or talk like Yoda you do, we can help you speak better!
EMPIRE SPEECH INSTITUTE Comlink Channel 3648
"Speak or speak not — there is no try!"

EMPLOYMENT

Job Opportunities

TIE FIGHTER PILOTS NEEDED
To fly around space station, get shot at by X-wing Fighters.
IMMEDIATE OPENINGS Contact: Grand Moff Tarkin c/o Death Star

X-WING FIGHTER PILOTS NEEDED
To fly around space station, get shot at by TIE Fighters.
IMMEDIATE OPENINGS Contact: Gold Leader, Rebel Forces

Job Opportunities

BOUNTY HUNTERS NEEDED
Short-term, part-time, long-term. Must be comfortable with both scum AND villainy. No long hair.
Contact: Admiral Piett, c/o Imperial Star Destroyer Executor

APPRENTICES WANTED
Interested in the Dark Side of the Force? Looking for an internship that'll get you college credit? Prominent Sith Lord is looking for a few dedicated students. Benefits include black cloaks, red lightsabers, and the name "Darth." Contact: ~~Supreme Chancellor Palpatine~~ Darth Sidious

HOUSING

Sales

Slimy! Mudhole! My home this is! (But yours it can be!) For over 900 years have I lived in this spacious 2BR hut complete with:
- Wood-burning stove
- Roomy 2 1/2' Ceilings
- Swamp-side views
800,000 Credits or Best Offer CONTACT: Dagobah Realty Ask for Yoda

You truly belong among the clouds ... and now you can be!
CLOUD CITY CONDOMINIUMS
Every apartment features:
- Dining room with killer views
- Living room with killer views
- Imperial torture chamber with killer electro-rack
AVAILABLE NOW 500,000 credits and up! Lando Calrissian Real Estate www.Calrissian.emp

MUSICIANS

CANTINA BAND
3 Piece Cover Band Knows Your Favorite Hits: "Lapti Nek," "Imperial March," "In Da Club," "Chicken Dance" * Weddings * Wookiee Life Day Celebrations * No Bar Mitzvahs *
Comlink 399272

JOB TRAINING

LEARN TO TEND BAR
Earn extra $$ while working in exotic locations:
Tatooine Cantina Downtown Coruscant Jabba's Sail Barge
* 1- or 2-week training
* Creatures with 6 or more arms a plus!
IMPERIAL BARTENDING INSTITUTE

MEDICAL SERVICES

PSYCHOLOGICAL COUNSELING
Is your father trying to kill you? Does your Wookiee always roar when you ask him to do the simplest tasks? Did that princess you fooled around with turn out to be your sister?
* Individuals * Couples * * Families * Children * Droids *
Dr. R7-D5,
Licensed Intergalactic Clinical Therapist
Empire Medical Plan Accepted Comlink 239823

HAND REPLACEMENT
I specialize in post-lightsaber injuries — whether it's hands or entire arms, lower bodies, legs, torsos, even heads!
Dr. 2-1B, Medical Droid Comlink 227756

MIDI-CHLORIAN SCREENING
Precise midi-chlorian count reveals just how powerful you are with the Force. Find out if you're a Jedi Knight ... or a Jedi Nobody. Fast, 24-hour turnaround. CONFIDENTIAL! www.MidichlorianClinic.jed

ARTIST: TOM BUNK

WRITER: DAVID SHAYNE

MAD #455, July 2005
"If the *Star Wars* Galaxy Had Classified Ads"

HERE WE GO WITH ANOTHER RIDICULOUS
MAD FOLD-IN

Right now several vicious fights are underway in the deepest reaches of space. Although all of them are sure to be violent, one in particular will stand out in its savagery. To find out which one will be a true bloodbath, fold page in as shown.

FOLD PAGE OVER LIKE THIS!

▲ Ⓐ   FOLD PAGE OVER LEFT   Ⓑ FOLD BACK SO THAT "A" MEETS "B"

YODA vs. SIDIOUS

MACE vs. GRIEVOUS

ANAKIN vs. OBI-WAN

THE REPUBLIC vs. THE SEPARATISTS

THE ONE WE MEAN ISN'T ON TELEVISION AND IT'S NOT BETWEEN
XBOX OR PLAYSTATION 2. THIS IS NOT AN EXAM AND
YOU DON'T HAVE TO GUESS. BUT IF YOU,
SIR OR MADAM, HAVE THE ANSWER, YOU'RE A GENIUS
SAVANT. IT'S USELESS ASKING PEOPLE OF LESS INTELL-
IGENCE. BY DOING THAT WE WOULD ONLY INVITE
RADICALLY CRAZY, WILD GUESSES. STUPID ONES, TOO

Ⓐ   ARTIST AND WRITER: AL JAFFEE   Ⓑ

NO NEED TO RUIN
YOUR BOOK BY
FOLDING THIS PAGE!
JUST TURN TO THE
NEXT PAGE TO SEE
THE ANSWER!

MAD #454, June 2005
Fold-in, "Which Epic Space Battle Will Prove to Be the Bloodiest?"

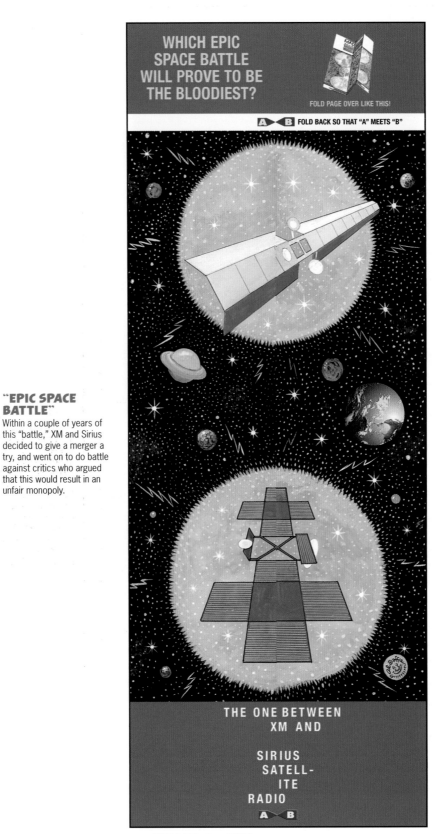

"EPIC SPACE BATTLE"
Within a couple of years of this "battle," XM and Sirius decided to give a merger a try, and went on to do battle against critics who argued that this would result in an unfair monopoly.

MAD #454, June 2005
Fold-in FOLDED!

TITLES GEORGE LUCAS
CONSIDERED FOR THE NEXT
STAR WARS MOVIE

★ **Star Wars: Episode III** — *Yoda Has A Bake Sale*
★ **Star Wars: Episode III** — *Dancin' in the Darth*
★ **Star Wars: Episode III** — *I See Dead Prequel*
★ **Star Wars: Episode III** — *Sith Happens*
★ **Star Wars: Episode III** — *Harold and Jar-Jar Go To White Castle*
★ **Star Wars: Episode III** — *Tatooine Idol*
★ **Star Wars: Episode III** — *How Yoda Got His Groove Back*
★ **Star Wars: Episode III** — *Crouching Jedi, Hidden Gungan*
★ **Star Wars: Episode III** — *Pimp My Millennium Falcon*
★ **Star Wars: Episode III** — *Revenge Of The Licensed Merchandise*
★ **Star Wars: Episode III** — *Dude, Where's My Death Star?*
★ **Star Wars: Episode III** — *My Big Fat Sith Wedding*

WHOEVER WINS... LUCAS GETS RICHER.

STAR WARS
EPISODE III
EWOK vs. PREDATOR
EVP

★ **Star Wars: Episode III** — *I'm Darth James, Bitch!*
★ **Star Wars: Episode III** — *Inherit the Windu*
★ **Star Wars: Episode III** — *The Windus of War*
★ **Star Wars: Episode III** — *Gone With The Windu*
★ **Star Wars: Episode III** — *The Sith Sense*
★ **Star Wars: Episode III** — *Droid Rage*
★ **Star Wars: Episode III** — *I, Droid*
★ **Star Wars: Episode III** — *A Space Odyssey*
★ **Star Wars: Episode III** — *Barbie and Kenobi*
★ **Star Wars: Episode III** — *Darth Maul of America*
★ **Star Wars: Episode III** — *The Passion of the Wookiee*

STAR WARS
EPISODE III
SCOOBY-DOOKU

★ **Star Wars: Episode III** — *Jedis of the Caribbean*
★ **Star Wars: Episode III** — *The Force for Dummies*
★ **Star Wars: Episode III** — *The Princess Amidala Diaries*
★ **Star Wars: Episode III** — *In Search of Harrison Ford*
★ **Star Wars: Episode III** — *Mission Accomplished!*
★ **Star Wars: Episode III** — *Not Another Palpatine Movie*
★ **Star Wars: Episode III** — *The Seven Habits of Highly Effective Sand-People*
★ **Star Wars: Episode III** — *Men Are From Coruscant, Women Are From Alderaan*
★ **Star Wars: Episode III** — *The Phantom Weapons of Mass Destruction*
★ **Star Wars: Episode III** — *The Return of Mr. Billy Dee Williams*
★ **Star Wars: Episode III** — *The Perfect Stormtrooper*
★ **Star Wars: Episode III** — *Harry Potter and the Prisoners of Naboo*
★ **Star Wars: Episode III** — *The Scent of a Wookiee*

STAR.WARS
EPISODE III
there's something about
jarjar

"THE SITH SENSE"
MAD didn't know that it was in the works when this piece was written, but as part of its *Revenge of the Sith* tie-in, Burger King had a website called sithsense.com where Darth Vader asked visitors to think of an animal, vegetable, or mineral. He then essentially played Twenty Questions to guess the answer, claiming to have read the visitor's mind by using the Force.

MAD #447, November 2004
"Titles George Lucas Considered for the Next *Star Wars* Movie"

COLORING WITHOUT COLOR

Artist Hermann Mejia is actually color-blind. He figures out color by working with an extensive tablet on which he has samples of different shades of color labeled. He then uses this tablet as a guideline when he paints. Or his wife just tells him what to do. Either way, it seems to work.

IMPERIAL WALKER CAMEO

Note the Imperial walker in the background, to the right of Senator AmaDilly. Hermann Mejia loves these vehicles and likes to slip them in his articles. You may have noticed one in "A Day in the Life of George Lucas." He also slipped one in among the elephant-like Mûmakil in *MAD's Lord of the Rings: The Return of the King* parody, "Bored of the Rings: The Rehash of the Thing."

Hermann Mejia's Imperial walker mixed in amongst the Mûmakil.
From *MAD* #440, April 2004.

CAUSE OF DARTH DEPT.
A long time ago (1977, to be exact), in a galaxy far, far away (or, to be more precise, Northern California), a young director named George Lucas released a trilogy of movies that people loved! But not content with the bazillions he made on the first three flicks, Lucas decided to crank out a new trilogy of prequels that people...um, well, hated! Why? Because even though the budgets and special effects went up, the writing and acting went way, way down! And this is the worst one of them all! In fact, it's...
STAR BORES
EPIC
RETREAD
We have to stop Count Cuckoo and General Greasy! They've kidnapped Chancellor Palpitation! Barf More, lock in the shields, we're flying directly into enemy fire!
Bloop-deep! (TRANSLATION: But Oldie Von Moldie, the ship could sustain a lot of damage!)
That's okay! The ship's a rental! And I sprung for the "Hit By Laser Cannons" insurance waiver!
In this Clone War, your help we will need, Chewing-Tobacco!
GGRRRRRAWGH! (TRANSLATION: Master Yodel, I would be honored to serve as a brave soldier!)
Actually, more as a new fur coat for me I was thinking! Cold it is aboard these battle ships! Purple have my green nipples turned!
Bar Stool, even though I could just land, I'm going to do a 360 degree spin, bank left, swoop right, then a 720 degree turn, fly between those two ships, zig, zag, then zig again, swoop up and THEN fly to the docking bay!
Bweeep-boop! (TRANSLATION: Why do you make things needlessly complicated? It only increases the chance of crashing!)
I can't help it! It's my training!
Beep-blop! (TRANSLATION: Your Jet-eye training?)
Job training! I used to work as a programmer for Microsoft!
BWWWARRRRRF!
With my Jet-eye powers, I sense a disturbance in the Force, Senator AmaDilly!
That "disturbance" was me puking all over the place! I have morning sickness!
Yes! I sense you have the stomach flu!
No, as I just told you, I have morning sickness! I'm pregnant!
No, I sense that it's stomach flu!
And I sense that you're an idiot!
HERMANN

MAD #456, August 2006
"Star Bores: Epic Load III Retread of the Sh*t!"

BAKER IN A CAN
Note that once the astromech droid's dome has popped off, a Kenny Baker look-alike is revealed to be inside. (Baker, of course, was the actor inside R2-D2.)

COUGH SYRUP
If you look closely, you'll notice that for the hacking, wheezing, and coughing General Greasy, Mejia provided a bottle of Robitussin.

THE EMPEROR AS THE GODFATHER

According to Episode II screenwriter Jonathan Hales, George Lucas's initial inspiration for the Emperor was not Don Corleone but rather Richard Nixon. In fact, as can be seen in J. W. Rinzler's *The Making of Star Wars: The Definitive Story Behind the Original Film*, Lucas's notes from circa 1974 show that the Empire was based at least in part on the activities of the Nixon regime, employing "Nixonian gangsters" for various nefarious deeds.

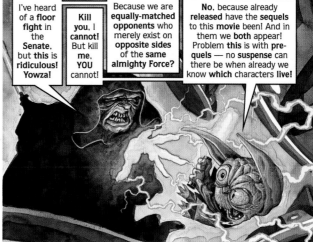

YODA THE CHIHUAHUA

Mejia's depiction of Yoda in this parody was inspired by Ren the Chihuahua from *The Ren & Stimpy Show*.

DARTH VADER CHEST PLATE GAG

Throughout *MAD*'s *Star Wars* parodies, "the Usual Gang of Idiots" have run different gags on Darth Vader's chest plate. Harry North, for example, put a telephone keypad there. Mort Drucker drew an image of Miss Piggy, and here Hermann Mejia puts in a 1980s-era cassette-based Walkman deck. Mejia did this because *Star Wars* reminded him of being a child in the late 1970s and early 1980s (the Walkman was introduced in 1979). ILM veterans Don and Anna Bies have, in fact, on Lucasfilm's behalf, slipped unique secret codes into the chest plate lettering of various Darth Vader costumes they constructed for public appearances. This was done so that anyone photographing the costume in an attempt to create a counterfeit one would unwittingly put one of these codes on the chest plate, and Lucasfilm could thus identify the forgery. A devious plot the Emperor himself would be proud of!

BIG HELMET

Mejia gave Traitor/Vader a big helmet here as a tip of the hat to Mel Brooks's Vader parody, Dark Helmet.

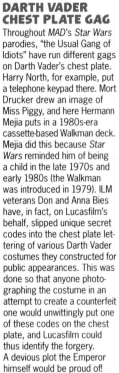

"FORCED" LAUGHTER

"THE FORCE-SKIN IS STRONG ON THIS ONE!"
Difficult circumcision is a recurring *MAD* favorite. I, myself, am guilty of such a gag in "What If Superman Were Raised by Jewish Parents" in *MAD* #325, February 1994.

MAD #459, November 2005
"'Forced' Laughter"
(Writer: Jason Reich; Artist: Al Jaffee)

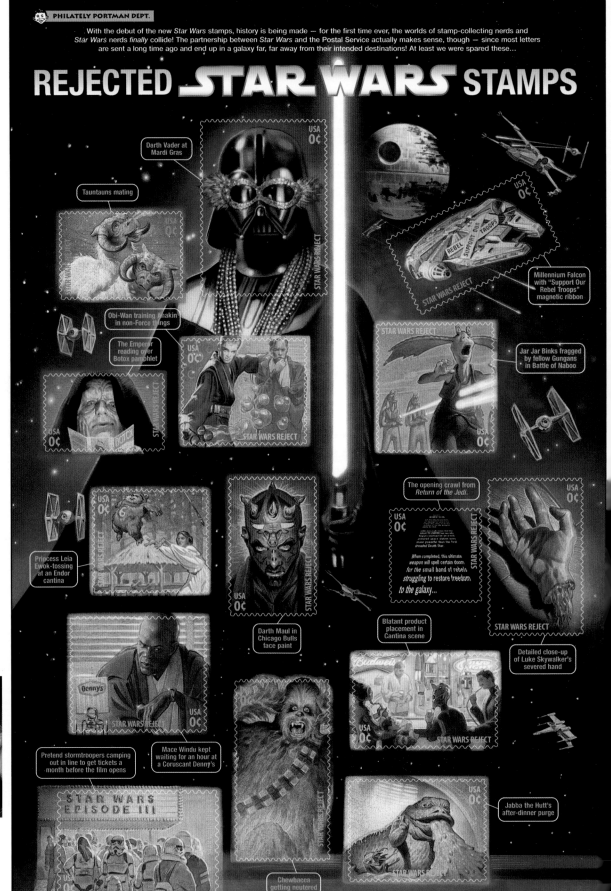

With the debut of the new *Star Wars* stamps, history is being made — for the first time ever, the worlds of stamp-collecting nerds and *Star Wars* nerds *finally* collide! The partnership between *Star Wars* and the Postal Service actually makes sense, though — since most letters are sent a long time ago and end up in a galaxy far, far away from their intended destinations! At least we were spared these...

REJECTED STAR WARS STAMPS

Darth Vader at Mardi Gras

Tauntauns mating

Millennium Falcon with "Support Our Rebel Troops" magnetic ribbon

Obi-Wan training Anakin in non-Force things

The Emperor reading over Botox pamphlet

Jar Jar Binks fragged by fellow Gungans in Battle of Naboo

Princess Leia Ewok-tossing at an Endor cantina

The opening crawl from *Return of the Jedi.*

Detailed close-up of Luke Skywalker's severed hand

Darth Maul in Chicago Bulls face paint

Blatant product placement in Cantina scene

Pretend stormtroopers camping out in line to get tickets a month before the film opens

Mace Windu kept waiting for an hour at a Coruscant Denny's

Jabba the Hutt's after-dinner purge

Chewbacca getting neutered

WRITER: JEFF KRUSE
ARTIST: MARK STUTZMAN

"JABBA THE HUTT'S AFTER-DINNER PURGE"

Lucasfilm actually licensed a vomit-capable Jabba toy that Hasbro released as part of its Episode I product line. Called "Jabba Glob," it was a hollow Jabba that could be filled with green slime and little plastic frogs. The idea was that when Jabba's head was squeezed, a little bit of the slime/frog mixture would ooze out of his mouth. However, as fans soon found out, Jabba could easily be made to puke if just a little more pressure was applied.

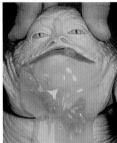

The charming "Jabba Glob" toy.
Photo by Anne Neumann.

MAD #479, July 2007
"Rejected *Star Wars* Stamps"

THE *MAD STAR WARS* CELEBRITY YEARBOOK

Over the years, various *Star Wars* celebrities have foolishly tarnished their careers by being willing to pose with an issue of *MAD*. Here is the photographic evidence of their dalliances with the "dork side."

Ray Park
Photo by Dave Croatto.

George Lucas
Photo by Jonathan Bresman.

Peter Mayhew
Photo by Dave Croatto.

Frank Oz
Photo by Jonathan Bresman.

***MAD* editor Nick Meglin and Mark Hamill**
Photo by John Ficarra.

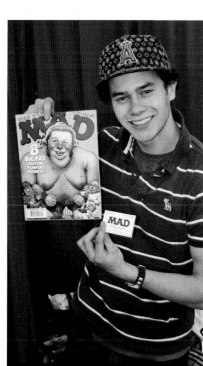

Daniel Logan
Photo by Dave Croatto.

Hayden Christensen and Rick McCallum
Photo by Jonathan Bresman.

ACKNOWLEDGMENTS

Special thanks to everyone who helped make this book possible:

Sue Adler
John Alcantar
Sergio Aragonés
Matthew Azeveda
Kenny Baker
Robert Barnes
Barbara Bellanca
Ahmed Best
Jason Best
Don Bies
Trisha Biggar
Mike Blanchard
Roger Bonas
Leonard Brenner
Alice Bresman
Dan Bresman
Joe Bresman
Bonnie Burton
Ben Burtt
Peg Burtt
Christine Cabello
Roberta Cairney
Ilkay Can
Tracy Cannobbio
Chris Cerasi
Stacy Cheregotis
Sonia Choi
Keith Clayton
David Craig
Dave Croatto
Dorothy Crouch
Anthony Daniels
Dick DeBartolo
Jo Donaldson
Barbara Drucker

Mort Drucker
Brian Durniak
Patty Dwyer
Carlo Eugster
Al Feldstein
John Ficarra
Hadley Fitzgerald
Ryan Flanders
Jim Fletcher
Alyson Forbes
Maureen Forster
Tom Forster
Mary Franklin
Warren Fu
Sid Ganis
Amy Gary
Joshua Greene
Maren Greif
Greg Grusby
Lynne Hale
Jonathan Hales
Keith Hamshere
Kristine Hanna
Erin Haver
Pablo Hidalgo
Andrew Howick
Alex Jaeger
Duncan Jenkins
Laura Jorstad
Charlie Kadau
Arie Kaplan
Dov Kelemer/DKE Toys
Robert Kempe
John Knoll
Charlie Kochman

Jay Kogan
Arnie Kogen
Steve Korté
Kristine Krueger
Halina Krukowski
Peter Kuper
Paul Kupperberg
Koichi Kurisu
Ellen Moon Lee
Linda Lee
Greg Leitman
Stacey Leong
Jake Lloyd
Lawreen Loeser
Daniel Logan
Justin Lubin
Jay Maidment
Angie Mayhew
Peter Mayhew
Iain McCaig
Rick McCallum
Bridget McGoldrick
Nick Meglin
Hermann Mejia
Evan Metcalf
Tina Mills
Rachel Milstein
Jennie Morel
Bill Morrison
Anne Neumann
Tony Overman
Frank Oz
Richard Palermo
Ray Park
Miles Perkins

David Perkinson
Lorne Peterson
Joel Press
Ardees Rabang
Joe Raiola
Jonathan Rinzler
Roel Robles
Carol Roeder
Howard Roffman
Sue Rostoni
Steve Sansweet
Darcy Savit
Irving Schild
Erich Schoeneweiss
David Shayne
Jay Shuster
Tom Silvestro
Nadina Simon
John Singh
Scott Sonneborn
David Stevenson
Erica Stimac
Michael Sutfin
Doug Thomson
Leslie Unger
Pete Vilmur
Sam Viviano
Dennis vonGalle
Amy Vozeolas
Jim Ward
Lucy Autrey Wilson
Stacey Witcraft
Monte Wolverton
Michael Wooten
Nellie Zupancic

And of course, a special thank-you to George Lucas for taking thirty years of *MAD*'s skewering in stride.

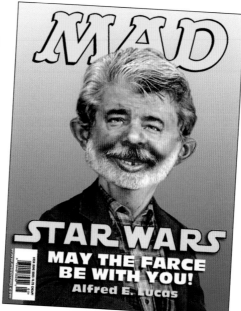

MAD #454, June 2005
The Cover We *Didn't* Use
(Artist: Sam Viviano)

ABOUT THE AUTHOR

Jonathan Bresman is *MAD* Magazine's senior editor in charge of developing new talent. What has he done to deserve such a punishment? Well in previous incarnations, he's served as a conceptual researcher on *Star Wars:* Episode I *The Phantom Menace*, as www.starwars.com's production correspondent, and as the author of the book *The Art of Star Wars:* Episode I *The Phantom Menace*. Bresman was also creative director of Vis-a-vis/Kerplink, an animation and design firm where he co-created award-winning cartoon properties. Additionally, he supervised concept design projects for clients such as Mainframe, Hasbro, and LeapFrog, and e-learning animations for companies such as Oracle, Pfizer, and Autodesk. Back in his undergraduate days at Harvard, Bresman interned for *The Late Show with David Letterman*, Lucasfilm, *MAD*, Marvel Comics, and Valiant Comics, and studied animation writing at the American Film Institute's Television Writers Workshop. He also has a master's degree in Communication and Education from Columbia University's Teachers College. His hobbies include taking nerdy photos with fictional characters.

Photo by Roel Robles.